One Green Mesquite Tree

by Gisela Jernigan

Illustrated by E. Wesley Jernigan

Harbinger House, Inc.

Tucson

One green mesquite tree
growing in the sun.
Two cicadas buzzing:
summer has begun!

Three tall saguaros
    bursting into bloom.
Four purple martins
    looking for some room.

Five jumping chollas
needle-sharp with thorns.
Six lively cactus wrens
chuckling in the morn.

Seven palo verdes
    form a golden bower.
Eight busy bumblebees
    drinking from the flowers.

Nine ocotillos
blossoms flaming red.
Ten emerald hummingbirds
coming to be fed.

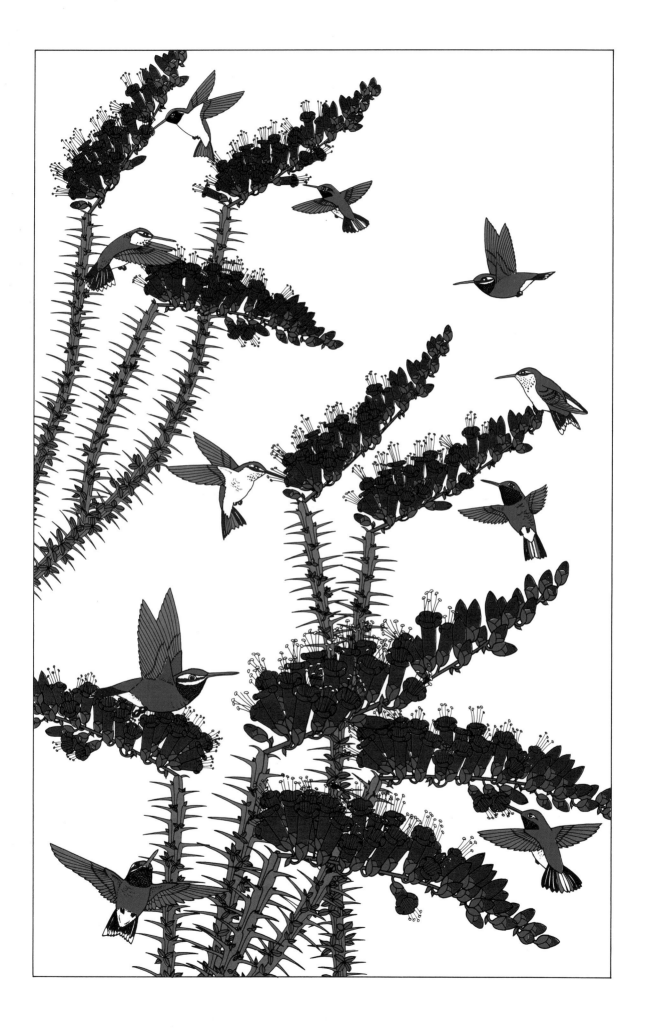

11

Eleven broad prickly pears
with fruit of flavor sweet.
Twelve desert tortoises
plodding up to eat.

12

Thirteen fragrant yuccas
  with flowers creamy white.
Fourteen yucca moths
  come lay their eggs at night.

Fifteen devil's claws,
    seed pods sharp and curved.
Sixteen bighorn sheep
    spread them with their fur.

Seventeen creosotes
    have little water needs.
Eighteen kangaroo rats
    make moisture from their seeds.

Nineteen barrel cacti
   crowned with fruits of yellow.
Twenty long-nosed bats
   seek them in the shadow.

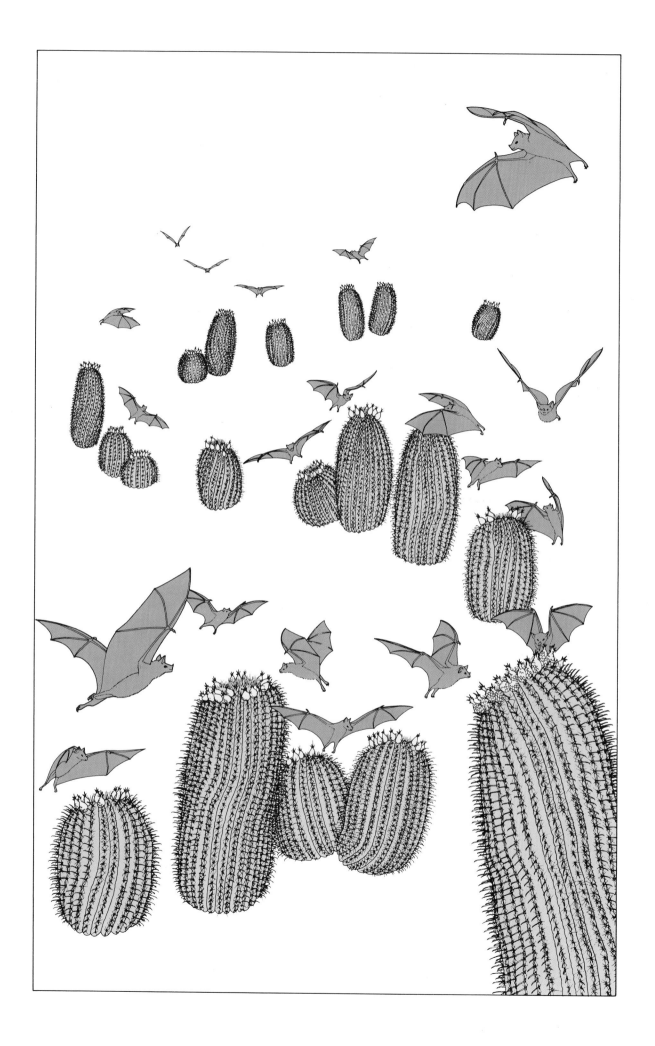

Glossary

Barrel cacti   Shaped like barrels, these cacti store water in their inner chambers.

Bighorn sheep   Wild sheep that live in rugged desert mountains.

Cactus wrens   Birds with unusual calls; they like to nest in cacti.

Cicadas (si-kay´-dah)   Heat-loving, tree-dwelling insects that make a loud humming, buzzing noise.

Creosotes (kree´-oh-sote)   Pungent shrubs that are the most common plants in the Sonora Desert.

Desert tortoises   Large, endangered reptiles that eat grasses and prickly pear fruits and pads.

Devil's claws   A shrub named for its claw-shaped seed pods that sometimes latch onto the fur and feet of animals.

Hummingbirds   Small birds that are especially attracted to red flowers and their nectar.

Jumping chollas (choy´-ah)   Spiny cacti with loose joints that are easily detached.

Kangaroo rats   High-jumping, seed-eating rodents that need very little water.

Long-nosed bats   Their long tongues and snouts help them feed on cactus nectar and fruit.

Mesquite (mess-keet´)   A tree belonging to the pea family, bearing edible beans.

Ocotillos (oh-ko-tee´-oh)   Thorny shrubs also called candlewood because of their bright red flower clusters.

Palo verdes (pal´-oh ver´-day)   "Green sticks" in Spanish, these spiny, green-branched trees belong to the pea family.

Prickly pears   Jointed cacti with flat pads and sweet edible fruit.

Purple martins   Birds that often nest in woodpecker holes in saguaros.

Saguaros (sa-war´-oh)   Tall, treelike cacti with branches that look like arms.

Yuccas (yuk´-ah)   Palmlike plants with one or more fragrant clusters of waxy, white flowers.

Yucca moths   Small, silver white moths that lay their eggs in yucca flowers.

what others feel, even when they are trying to hide their feelings or hide from them.

Mother and Almah have each told me about the first months of my life, when the army was looking for Habiru male babies. I do not remember that, of course. But I still remember the silence of Abba and Ima was as powerful as the jaws of a crocodile. Their fear was as cold and deep as the Great Green Sea, and it closed my throat so tightly that I could not cry, even when I was hungry.

Almah said I never made a happy sound until Mother held me the first time. I remember the smell of sun and wind on soft warm skin and the feeling that I was safe at last. Most of all I remember listening to Mother's heart singing. I did not know that is what hearts are supposed to do, until she pressed me against hers.

Ima never talked of those times. She spoke only about Ya and our ancestors. I have never been able to know her feelings. It is as if she is made of stone and her feelings are buried deep like the mummies of the pharaohs of ancient times that are hidden in the secret chambers of the pyramids. I know her feelings are there, but I do not know what they are. Maybe all her feelings belong to Ya, because she has never talked of much else to me.

"Why you speak so much of Ya?" I asked her once.

She frowned. I knew it was not my question that bothered her but the way I spoke. It has always bothered her. When I was still a child she told me, "You talk like you are ignorant. You don't have to talk like that. Why do you?"

I did not know how to explain to her that words feel like stones in my mouth. I do not like words and do not trust them. I know I sound sometimes like I am not very intelligent. In my mind words flow like the Hapi. But when they reach my tongue, they start to go backward, as if they do not want to leave me, as if they do not want anyone to hear them except me. It is hard to talk about that to someone as sure of her opinions as Ima. So I said nothing that day. I have never said much when I'm with her, which is not often these days.

"I did not talk about Ya enough to your sister, and look what happened," she said finally, in answer to my question. "She forgot who she was. She betrayed us and she betrayed Ya."

But Almah did not forget and she betrayed no one. She simply does not believe. I wonder if Ima would understand if she saw Almah dance at a festival. Grandfather says Almah causes the goddesses to walk among the people. Ima could not see that because she does not believe in goddesses. That is why she and Almah cannot talk to each other. Neither believes what the other believes.

It is Shemu, Harvest Season. The river is at its lowest, and almost everyone in Khemet works in the fields, harvesting the grain and vegetables, even those like Abba and Aharon who ordinarily work building the temples.

When the harvest is done, I will start going outside the palace grounds again during the day. It never bothered me, until this year. Now I am terrified that if I go outside I will see Aharon, Abba, Ima, and Miryam sweating in the fields. I am terrified they will look up and see me and hate me. I am afraid all of the Habiru will see me and hate me. But they probably do already.

I am Habiru. I should be out there with them. But I don't want to be. I am glad I don't have to work in the hot sun all day getting my hands dirty, and my body becoming smelly and slick with sweat. And I hate myself for feeling like this. But I am glad I am not a slave.

I wish I could talk to someone. Kakemour would not understand. Almah understands me better than anybody, but she is a priestess. She knows who she is. I feel as if I will never know who I am.

If I could be anybody in Khemet, I wish I could be Almah. I don't think even Grandfather is as happy to be who he is as Almah is to be a priestess and dance naked at the temple.

"Why don't you believe in Ya?" I asked her once.

"Ya does not make me want to dance. When I dance, the people see that Hathor and Eset are real. When I think about Ya, I do not feel like dancing. This is what I was born to do, Mosis."

"What was I born to do, Almah?"

She hugged me to her. "I don't know. You will find out one day."

I was ten the first time I saw her dance. It was during the festival of Hathor, protector of women and the goddess of dance, love, and joy. We were outside the Great Temple in Pi-Ramesses. Its columns are so tall that even now I have to bend my head all the way back to see to the top. Unlike other temples, whose outside walls are

91

carved with scenes of Grandfather standing in his chariot, pulling a bow and arrow, and leading the charge against the Hittites at the Battle of Kadesh, the outside of the Great Temple is white and a large cow with stars in her belly—the goddess Hathor—is painted on it. Abba was one of the workmen who put the huge stones in place, and my brother, Aharon, helped paint the picture of the goddess.

I sat between Grandfather and Mother at the entrance to the temple, statues of a seated pharaoh on either side of us. From where we sat we could see all four sections of the city and their temples, each dedicated to a god or goddess—Wadjet ruled the northern section, Seth the south, Astarte the east, and Amon the west. The temples are taller than the other buildings, and because of their colorful walls of green, red, blue, and white and the pictures of the gods or goddesses painted on them— regardless of where you are in the city—you have only to raise your eyes and you will be reminded of *maat* and that your life and everything you do helps create divine order.

I liked sitting above the people, liked that they were looking up and pointing excitedly at Ramesses, and I imagined them wondering who the boy was sitting next to him. I was on his right and Mother was next to me. Intef and Kakemour sat on the other side, where Queen Nefertari would have sat if she had been alive. Almah told me that there had been another queen, Asetnefret, but no one seemed to know where she was or what had happened to her.

Below us was the temple porch, where the dancing would be. Below the porch, at the bottom of the broad steps leading up to it, the mass of people extended as far as I could see along the Avenue of Hathor, which led to the temple. Round columns, sixty feet high, bordered both sides of the street. Images of the gods and goddesses had been cut into each one, and from where I sat, the carvings looked like the shadows of leaves flickering against tree bark. Beneath the columns the people were smaller and less consequential than half-completed thoughts. On the first, sixth, seventh, fifteenth, and twenty-third of each month, there was a festival. No one worked on those days, and people could eat and drink as much as they wanted, the meat and beer a gift of the pharaoh.

At the first jingling sound of the *shesheset*, everyone quieted. The person shaking it could not be seen, but the sound signaled that the dancing was about to begin. The *shesheset* is a long-handled instrument holding an oblong frame, inside of which are metal disks threaded onto small rods. A soft musical sound is made when it is shaken. I had seen Almah's *shesheset* many times in her suite. It was made especially for her because she is the priestess of Hathor. There is only one like it. Larger than the ordinary ones, it is of fine gold, so that it constantly flashes, sending light back to the sun even as it receives light. The head of Hathor is carved on each side of the handle, while the frame is shaped like the curved horns of a bull. Hathor was the mother of Amon-Re, the sun god, and she held the sun between her horns, and stars in her belly.

Even though I could not see who was shaking the *shesheset*, I knew from the sound it was Almah. The rhythm she was making with it filled me with a tension that became tighter and tighter until, just as I was ready to scream or shout or do something that would have been out of character, suddenly, from the right side of the porch, my sister leaped out, naked, the *shesheset* in her hand, the light from its gold flashing across our eyes in the rhythm of its beat.

Both Grandfather and Mother had told me Almah would be dancing that day, and I knew that the priestesses danced naked. People in Khemet do not wear many clothes, anyway. But this was my sister! I did not want her showing her body to everyone. I did not want all those eyes fixed on her as if she were a roasted bullock they were about to eat. Most of all, I did not want to look at her, even though I could not turn my eyes away.

But now the porch was filled with the sound of drums, and the music of flutes and horns as the musicians, all naked women, danced out from the opposite side and seated themselves at the back.

As I watched Almah leap and spin and somersault across the porch, something odd happened. I stopped seeing her as my sister, and she became someone who merely *looked* like my sister. I was enthralled by her beauty, her joy, her lack of self-consciousness, and no longer cared who she was. I cared only that she never stopped leaping and spinning to the beat of the drums, the *shesheset*, and the music of the flutes and horns.

My eyes widened and my heart beat faster as the

rhythms pounded at me like the heartbeat of the sun. I felt like I, too, wanted to dance, could dance—and more, *should*. The crowd below started clapping their hands in rhythm to the drums. I closed my eyes, and my body began swaying from side to side. Nothing existed anymore except the melodies and rhythms filling the air, and I thought I could feel the passion throbbing in the hearts of everyone in the crowd, and I, too, wanted to be naked and beautiful and to dance for the goddess, and I started to get up from my seat as my hands dropped to my hips to take off my kilt.

Suddenly Ima's face came into my mind like a funeral mask, and just like that, all the passion, joy, and love for the goddess that had been rising through my body like the sun reaching for midday were drowned in a sadness as bottomless as night. My body stopped moving and I stood still as if I had been turned into a statue. Then I slumped slowly into my seat, alone and empty.

I was a mere spectator now, watching a beautiful woman spinning in time to the music, which became faster—but no matter how fast the musicians played, she spun faster and leaped higher.

I happened to glance at Grandfather. His eyes had grown large and were fixed on Almah, and his mouth was open, his lips glistening with moisture. I was too young then to know the word *lust*, but I felt in him a yearning as broad and wide and deep as the Hapi when it has reached its height, a desire more intense than the sun on the sand and a hunger nothing could satisfy.

The music and drums played even faster and Almah

did a series of back flips and just as she disappeared from view, the music and rhythm stopped abruptly. All the people erupted into shouting and cheering and then they started chanting, "Meryetamun! Meryetamun! Meryetamun!"

I did not understand. "Why chant for you?" I asked Mother.

"That is your sister's Khemetian name," she said in a tight voice. After a pause, she continued in a voice that tried to sound cordial but was as empty of warmth as night in the desert. "The pharaoh gave it to her when she became a priestess." Mother was trying to hide something from me.

I still did not understand. "Grandfather give you new name?"

"No, but I am called Batya now."

I was confused. Batya was a Habiru name and meant "daughter of God."

"That is the name Yocheved gave me," Mother explained.

I was more confused. My sister, the Habiru, was a Khemetian priestess and had my mother's Khemetian name. My mother, the Khemetian, had a Habiru name given her by my and my sister's *ima*. And I, a Habiru, carried the name of an Egyptian god. I doubted I would ever understand.

Almah—for that is what I continued to call her—returned to the porch in answer to the chanting of her Khemetian name. Now, however, she wore a long white dress and looked like my sister. She turned and bowed to

96

the pharaoh. In what even I knew was a remarkable gesture, he rose and bowed to her. The cheers and shouting of the crowd became so loud when he did that, I expected the pillars of the temple to crumble.

But Mother was not cheering, and when I happened to glance at Kakemour, there was a look of hatred and anger on his face that frightened me.

SOON AFTER I SAW Almah dance for the first time, Grandfather invited me and Mother to eat with him. This was not unusual, as we ate with him at least once a week, and sometimes more. Often it was just the three of us, but sometimes other children of his would be there. Some were adults, while others were my age or younger. I am not sure even Grandfather knows how many children he has. I asked Kakemour once and he said sixty, but that was five years ago. I wanted to ask him how many wives and concubines Grandfather had but was too shy. All the wives, concubines, and their children live in special palaces in various parts of Khemet and visit Grandfather when he asks them to, which is often. Grandfather likes women and children.

That afternoon when we went for dinner, we were surprised to see Almah sitting on the floor next to Grandfather as comfortably as a cat who knows she will not be punished regardless of what she does.

Mother looked somberly at Almah. If Ima was as silent as the river and Almah shone like polished sunlight, Mother was as serious as words on stone. Of my three mothers, she is the one who wants to understand everything. Ima and Almah have more in common than they will ever admit, because neither questions what she knows. Mother questions even when she knows. When Ima told stories about our ancestors, she told them the same way every time. Mother couldn't tell a story without wanting to know why Ya did such-and-such. Abba and Mother seemed like they didn't care if they found the answers as much as they were happy to look for them. Almah and Mother used to be like sisters. Now Mother was Ima's daughter, while Ima and her real daughter had not seen each other since before I learned to walk.

Something happened when Mother's mother, Queen Nefertari, died. I was still an infant then, but I remember Mother's grief felt like a calf being skinned while still alive. Even now, fifteen years later, when Mother talks about her mother, my stomach burns from cuts that have not healed.

I think Grandfather wanted Mother and Almah to be friends again, but they sat across from each other more wary than two strange cats being asked to drink milk from the same bowl. Silence at the dinner table was something no Khemetian could tolerate, and Grandfather broke it by asking me to recite a hymn to Osiris and to read to him from a papyrus of the Book of the Dead. I did, and he was delighted by how well I recited and read. It is odd that when I recite a poem or read from a scroll, my tongue feels as fluid as a fish moving through water. If only someone would always give me the right words to say.

After we finished eating, Grandfather said he wanted to show us something. "I apologize for not having shown it to you before," he said to Mother, "for having kept it a secret. I wanted to keep it to myself, and that was selfish."

Neither of us knew what he was talking about. As we left the dining room, Almah slipped her arm inside Grandfather's with no more thought than it took to blink one's eyes. I did not have to look up to know that Mother had noticed, too, and was wondering.

Mother and I followed them from the dining room, down a corridor, and into a small room I had never seen. One wall was covered with a painting of the goddess Maat kneeling, her feathered arms outstretched. Just as I wondered if this was what Grandfather had wanted us to see, Almah pushed against something on the back wall. A door opened. A secret room!

Mother and I looked at each other, then followed Almah and Grandfather through the door and into a room whose four white walls were covered with pictures of the most beautiful woman I had ever seen. Mother gasped loudly and I knew whom I was looking at. Or did I? I thought the paintings were of Queen Nefertari, but how amazing! They looked like Almah.

In one she was holding a baby, and I wondered if it was supposed to be Mother. In another she was sitting in the garden of the Women's Palace where Almah liked to sit, geese and ibises flying overhead. On another wall she walked in the garden of the palace at Opet with Ramesses. I had never known her, but looking at those paintings, oh, how I missed her!

I wished Ima could see this, because she says Kheme-tians are in love with death. But that is not true. It is just the opposite. They love life so much they cannot bear to believe it ends with death. Looking at the paintings of Nefertari, I agreed. It was not right or fair that someone so beautiful and gracious should be dead. And she wasn't. At least not in this secret room.

Grandfather stared for the longest at each painting, sometimes reaching out to touch her face lightly with his fingertips. Almah stood beside him, and I had the feeling they had come to the room many times. She seemed to know when Grandfather had stayed long enough because I was feeling grief like sand being blown against one's cheeks during a storm but could not tell if the grief belonged to Grandfather or Mother until Almah put her arm through his again and moved him gently away from the images of his beloved and toward the door. Mother was sobbing quietly, but I could not tell if it was from seeing the pictures of her mother, or that Almah had known about this room and she had not, or that it was Almah's hand her father was holding and not her own.

Almah stood at the threshold, looking at the walls covered with pictures of the woman she looked like. Suddenly music poured from her voice through barely parted lips, making me feel pain and joy as sharp-edged as the last sliver of color before night sits on the throne of heaven. There were no words, only soft notes of music searching for life and finding only shadows. Then she stopped and silence swallowed the last reverberation of melody, leaving each of us alone.

Chapter Two

BBA'S HAIR AND BEARD are almost white now. His eyelids are puffy, and large folds of skin hang beneath his eyes, as if he has spent all his nights praying and his prayers have not been answered.

Abba sits on the couch next to me and takes a fig from the bowl offered him by a servant. Though I was not expecting him today, he has visited often in the three years since I've had my own suite. Sometimes he stays the night in Almah's suite down the hall because mine is small. Today, however, he has not come just to visit. Something is on his mind. I can't help wondering if he has come to ask me when I am going to acknowledge my true heritage and start working with him and Aharon. But that is probably just my guilt speaking. Ima might say that, but not Abba.

He chews noisily and I follow his eyes as he looks at the paintings on the walls. On the wall behind me is one of a crocodile with its mouth open, a reminder to me of the miracle of my life. To a Khemetian, however, it is a depiction of the god Sobek. Over Abba's shoulder is a scene of three women playing with a child, the only way I have devised of bringing my three mothers together. On the wall by the door leading to my bedroom a woman dances. It is not Almah, but that is who I think of when I look at it.

"So," Abba says in Habiru, his eyes finally coming to rest on my face, "why have you stopped coming to visit your mother?"

His words take me by surprise. I feel myself blushing. "Long time," I finally manage to say.

"Do you know how long?" Abba insists.

I do. I look down at the floor.

"How do you think your mother feels? It has been a year since her last-born child has been to see her. A year! Aharon and Miryam think you don't like them. Your mother is afraid you have become a traitor to your people. Like your sister."

My mouth moves as I search for an excuse, but not even the sound of anguish comes out. I have no excuse. How can I tell Abba that I do not like being around Ima, that I never have? Only Almah understands what it is like to be with your real mother and wish you were with almost anyone else in the world. I know I am not supposed to have these feelings and I wish I didn't. But I do.

Abba sighs and takes another fig from the bowl the servant left on the table. After more noisy chewing, he resumes talking. "I know you are not a traitor. Neither is your sister. But only you and I believe that. You remember the story of our forefather Yitzchak, his wife, Rivka, and their two sons, Yaakov and Esav?"

Of course. When Rivka was pregnant, Ya told her she was carrying twin boys and the one born first, Esav, would serve the younger twin, Yaakov. Years passed. Yitzchak was old and blind and thought he was going to die. He wanted to give Esav the inheritance, but Rivka found out. She disguised Yaakov to be like Esav, and Yitzchak gave Yaakov the inheritance by mistake.

"Sometimes one parent sees something in a child the other does not," Abba continues. "Parents have favorites. Avraham favored Yitzchak over Yishmael. Rivka favored Yaakov over Esav, and Yaakov favored Yosef over his other eleven sons. It is not right, but sometimes a parent sees himself in a child, or sees himself as he would like to be. Most of the time it is the child who looks at the parents and sees who he wants to be. But occasionally the parent lives through the child. Yitzchak was quiet; Esav was a hunter, a man of the outdoors, and that was the kind of man Yitzchak would have liked to have been. Because of that he could not see that Esav was not the one to whom he should pass responsibility for the knowledge of Ya, the one god, the god who cannot be seen because he is the creator of all the gods who can be seen. This was what the inheritance was. If Esav had received it, there would be no Habiru today. That is why Rivka tricked her husband. She knew a truth he did not."

Abba shakes his head. "The more white there is in my hair and beard, the less I understand. The more weariness in my eyes, the more I question whether I have made the right decisions."

He gets up and begins pacing slowly. "Yocheved blames me. She says if I had not taught Almah to speak Khemetian, things would be different. That is true. If I had not taught her Khemetian, she would not have been able to speak to the princess and you would not have been saved from the soldiers. However, if I had not taught her Khemetian, she would be living in Goshen, married, and teaching her children about Ya. But I saw something in your sister your mother did not."

"What?" I ask.

"The spark of holiness!"

I would not have thought of those words, but I think I understand.

"When I was a boy," he goes on, "my father would wake me to go to the roof with him and say the morning prayers as the sun rose. That is how his father taught him and how I thought I would teach my son. But my first child was a daughter. Maybe everything would be different if I had thought a woman could pray to Ya like a man. It never occurred to me.

"One morning as I came onto the roof, Almah was already there. She was only four or five. Her back was to me and she was facing east. I was about to say something, when she opened her arms as if commanding the sun to rise. And just then, it did, and its first rays flowed over her like a water of light. She stood perfectly still, her arms outstretched as if—as if she were a goddess. I could not believe I had such a thought, but she reminded me of paintings on the walls of the temples in Pi-Ramesses.

"When she lowered her arms I went to her and asked, 'What game were you playing?'

"She looked at me seriously and said, 'I wasn't playing.'

"I didn't ask her anything else. I didn't want to know. I never saw her do it again, and I came to the rooftop late for several mornings after that to watch her. But she was never there, though she wasn't asleep, either. I suspected she had found another place, a secret one, known only to her and the sun. That was when I began speaking to her in Khemetian. I don't know why I did. It seemed like the right thing, and the rapidity with which she learned made me wonder if Khemetian was really her first tongue."

I see a smile of pride on his lips as he relives the scene with his firstborn. Then he looks at me and his eyes shine with the avidity of conviction. "What I saw in Almah that morning was the courage to love holiness. Do you know how rare that is? It is one thing to follow all the rules that are supposed to make you holy. It is another to hug holiness to you. Yocheved *believes* in Ya and the special destiny he has promised our people. But she does not *love* the mystery of the sun rising. Your sister did. I had no idea what it meant. But I was convinced it was not wrong. As surely as Rivka knew that Yaakov was the true heir, I knew Almah understood holiness in a way I could not begin to imagine."

I nodded and glanced at the painting of the woman dancing.

"Don't ever let your sister know, but I come to almost every festival to watch her dance. I am still uncomfortable seeing her without clothing, but after a while I forget she is my daughter. All I see is a goddess." He chuckles. "And I don't believe in goddesses. Or maybe I do and am afraid to say so. You see, I do not have Almah's courage to love. Maybe that is why she is my favorite. Please don't be hurt by that."

I shake my head. "Mine, too."

He smiles. "So, perhaps both of us seek to live courage through her."

I return his smile, though weakly because I am wondering if I will ever have my own courage.

Abba hesitates, as if there is something more he wants me to know but is not sure if I am ready to hear it or if he is ready to say it. "Could I have a cup of wine?" he asks.

I ring the bell that is on the floor beside the couch, and when the servant comes in, I ask for a jug of wine and a cup. Abba is silent until after the servant returns, pours the wine, and leaves. He takes a long sip, swallows, and sighs with satisfaction.

"One time in my life I had courage. I think. It was fifteen years ago, a few months after you, Almah, and your *ima* came to live here. One afternoon as Aharon and I were going back to Goshen after working in Pi-Ramesses, Yocheved was waiting on the road, looking for me. I had never seen her so upset. I sent your brother on and came with your mother and sat under a tree on the grass outside the palace walls.

" 'You must do something about Almah,' she said. 'She has become the pharaoh's concubine.'

"I was shocked! My Almah? Yocheved swore it was true because the pharaoh had just that very morning given her baskets filled with golden bracelets, fine clothes, and a golden mirror that had belonged to his wife. And, if that were not bad enough, he had given her a suite of rooms of her own. 'No man gives a woman all that without expecting something in return.' She went on to say it was my fault that Almah refused to obey her any longer, so I had to make her go back to Goshen before it was too late.

"I refused to do anything until I talked to Almah. That made Yocheved even more angry. 'Don't you believe me?' she wanted to know. 'Don't you trust what I say?' I hate to say it, but the truth was I didn't trust Yocheved where Almah was concerned. I told her to get Almah.

"When Yocheved returned, a woman in a wig of long tight braids walked a few steps behind her. Her eyes, lips, and cheeks were painted, and golden bracelets were on her arms. She was wearing a dress of the finest linen, beneath which I could see the faintest outlines of her naked body. It was Almah! I couldn't believe my eyes, didn't want to believe them. Who knows what I would have done or said if Yocheved had not pointed at Almah and spat out, 'Here is the Pharaoh's whore!'

"Whatever shock and revulsion I may have felt looking at Almah, I knew as surely as I knew anything in my life that whatever Almah was doing or thought she was doing, she was not that. I looked at Almah. Her eyes were brimming with tears. I opened my arms and she rushed into them, and I held her to me as tightly as I could."

He stops and sips more wine. When he resumes, his voice cracks with pain suppressed. "Yocheved has never forgotten and never forgiven me. Fifteen years and she still looks at me as if I betrayed her. Perhaps I should not be telling you all this, but there is too much talk of Ya in our family and not enough about each other.

"I suppose I did betray her, but I *had* to protect Almah. Yocheved understands what it means to be obedient. She does not understand what it is to be a vessel for the holy. She pushed Almah out of my arms and shouted at her, 'If you do not go back to Goshen now, you will be dead to me. Your name will never pass my lips again, and I will not allow your name to be said in my presence. Choose. Ya or Pharaoh!'

"Though there were tears in Almah's eyes, there was also a calmness, the serenity of holiness. She looked at me. 'Which is it?' I asked her. Without thinking, I spoke to her in Khemetian. She answered, 'Look at me, Abba. Do you have to ask?'

"What was I supposed to have done? Was there something I could have done that would not have meant choosing my wife over my daughter, or my daughter over my wife? Fifteen years I have thought about that afternoon and have not found another answer. I looked at Yocheved and said, 'She chooses Pharaoh.' Yocheved's face muscles twitched as if I had slapped her.

"She didn't say a word but walked away from the palace and back to Goshen. She said the princess could get a wet nurse for you because that was all you needed her for. She and Almah have not seen each other since that day. Yocheved and I have never spoken of that afternoon, either. Nor have we spoken of much else. Fifteen years."

He is quiet for a long time. The light on the walls fades and a servant comes in to light the lamps.

Finally Abba continues. "To this day I do not know if I did the right thing. I have a daughter whose name is never mentioned. When the Teller recites the roll of the families and comes to the names of Amram and Yocheved and their children, Almah's name is not mentioned."

"Almah is good," I put in.

"But she is also a priestess of Hathor and Eset. We are Habiru and worship only Ya." Then he looks at me, his eyes as hard as hammered light. "And whom do you worship, Mosis?"

I shake my head and say nothing.

Chapter Three

ALMAH AND I HAVE DINNER together almost every night. Often she has to dance at a festival, attend a banquet with the pharaoh, or talk with a younger priestess who may be having a problem, so it will be late before she returns. But I am always here waiting for her. When I awake each morning, I like knowing that my day will end with Almah.

I am most myself when we are together because then I come closest to saying what I feel. Even if she does not always understand, she takes my words into her heart as if they were the notes of a bird's song at dawn. I do not have trouble talking when Almah is listening. I tell her about Abba's visit but leave out that he has seen her dance.

"How do you feel about going back to see Ima? Do you want to?" she wants to know, biting into a date.

"I never want to see Goshen again as long as I live. I hated it all those years Mother took me there once a week or so to visit. I hate to say it, but I don't have pleasant memories of Ima. She seems to enjoy seeing me forced to eat from straw bowls and dishes and speak Habiru. Both she and Mother were always telling me how important it was to get to know 'my people.' I don't have any 'people.' I feel closer to the servants and court officials and scribes. Aharon is less of an older brother to me than Kakemour, who taught me to use a bow and arrow, swords, a spear, and how to drive a horse and chariot."

Almah smiles sadly. "I am sorry it is so hard for you."

"You don't know how much I envy you," I say with anguish. "You haven't had to go to Goshen in fifteen years nor listen to Ima go on and on about Ya."

She nods. "That's true, but sometimes I miss her. She is my mother. Sometimes I wish she could see me dance even though she would hate it and me for doing it. Still, I think someplace deep down inside she would be proud of me, too." Almah laughs sadly. "No. I am wishing for something that will never be. That is not Ima. That is the *ima* I wish she were."

"Odd family," I say, and we laugh. "Think about it," I continue. "You were born Habiru but are so accepted by the Khemetians that people refer to me as often by the title Brother of the Priestess as they do Grandson of the Pharaoh. Mother, born Khemetian, is more accepted in Goshen than either you or I. She speaks fluent Habiru now and almost looks like one since she stopped wearing jewelry and makeup."

"But she won't let her hair grow out," Almah puts in, chuckling.

"No. Said she couldn't—yet. But she speaks of Ya as if he is her god."

"And who is your god, Mosis?" Almah asks quietly.

We are lying at opposite ends of a couch, our legs touching lightly, each of us cupping a bowl of sweet wine as the servants take away the dishes.

I shake my head. "Don't want to talk about it."

"I know. But perhaps you will know who you are once you know which god you serve."

I want to ask her something, but I am afraid of how I will feel if she does not say what I want to hear. But I have to know. I wonder if I will be able to serve any god until I do know.

"What's the matter?" she asks after the silence has gone on too long.

I look at her and then look away.

"Talk to me, Mosis."

"I'm afraid of what you might say."

"Might say about what?"

"Might say if I decide to serve Ya." My voice sounds so small in my ears I am not certain I have said anything aloud.

But I know I have when I hear Almah say, "Mosis, we don't have to agree for me to love you. I want you to be as happy serving the god you want to as I am serving the ones I do."

"Thank you. Thank you so much."

"Is that what you want to do? Serve Ya?"

I shake my head. "Don't know. That's the problem! Look at me. My eyelids are painted. My body is oiled. Gold bracelets on my wrists. It's ridiculous, but I feel naked if I don't have on jewelry. I like living here in the palace and going to banquets with Kakemour and meeting beautiful women. I enjoy that more than visiting Ima and hearing boring stories. And yet, you belong here. I don't. But I don't belong there, either."

She nods eagerly. "I do know what you mean. It is only because I belong to the goddess that I feel at home here. But otherwise, I feel somewhat like a stranger, too."

"But what about the pharaoh? You seem to be the one he wants closest to him. Almah?" I stop. There is something else I have been wanting to ask her for almost as long as I can remember. "Almah?"

"What is it, Mosis?"

"Do you— Have you—?"

She smiles. "No, I do not sleep with Ramesses. I never have. He wanted to make me his wife once."

"Are you serious?" I exclaim. "You might have been Great Royal Wife? Why didn't you?"

"I don't know if he would have made me Great Royal Wife. But Ramesses did not need to make me his wife to help him assuage his grief for Nefertari. He loves me, yes. But what he loves more is looking at me and seeing her. What woman wants to live as a substitute for one who is dead? No, I belong to the goddess, and that is why the people love me so. Because no man can have me, then I belong to everyone—men and women. But sometimes I wish you and I were truly Khemetian and had been born into the royal family. Then we could marry each other."

I blush.

"I'm sorry. Maybe I shouldn't have said that."

"No. No. I'm glad you did. I've thought it enough

times." Still, I am not comfortable talking about it anymore and look for a way to change the subject. "But all we've done is talk about me. What about you? How're things with you?"

"Well, I'm not sure. I mean, I'm fine, but maybe I should tell you and see what you think."

"About what?"

"For the past week or so I have been feeling that Intef, Kakemour, and Ramesses are planning something, and they want to keep it a secret from me. Whenever I enter the throne room, they stop talking. That has never happened. Maybe it's nothing. But I don't like it, Mosis. I thought they trusted me. Now I am not sure, and it hurts."

"You are worried."

"Yes, I am. I have to find out what they're planning. Maybe you can help."

"How?" I ask, unable to think of what I could do.

"I know I'm probably being silly, but would you talk to Batya? She might know something. Would you talk to her?"

"Of course, but what could she know?"

"Probably nothing, but I don't know what else to do."

THE NEXT MORNING Mother appears just as I am finishing breakfast. We embrace. She looks at me and I at her because we have not seen each other in a long time. I had almost forgotten how much I love this face from which goodness shines like fire.

"It has been too long," she says hesitantly, sitting on a couch.

"Yes."

"How have you been?"

She is the only person I know who asks that question in such a way that you know she is not inquiring about your physical well-being.

I shake my head. "I am not sure."

"What's the matter?"

"I'm fifteen. No wife. No children. I don't do anything. I don't fit anywhere. If Grandfather died, I would be thrown into the street. Look at me! I walk and talk and dress like a Khemetian, but I am not. You are more Habiru than I am!"

"Mosis." Her voice is quiet, but there is so much strength in it. When I was little I believed that if she spoke to a crocodile, it would close its jaws and ask her to forgive it for being a crocodile. "Yocheved and I have wondered, too, wondered why Ya would want a Habiru boy brought up in the palace of the pharaoh."

"Do you know?"

"I may. I just may."

"Tell me, please."

"Do you ever think about your ancestor Yosef?"

"No. Not really."

"Perhaps you should. He was even more lonely than you. You have always known your family. He was taken from his when he was seventeen and sold into Khemet as a slave. He rose to become the second most powerful man in all the land. And yet he never forgot Ya. He never forgot he was Habiru. There was no one to remind him of this. Yet he remembered."

She does not have to say the rest: I have forgotten. I drop my head to my chest.

"I am glad your *ka* is troubled," she continues. "I was afraid I would come to you and you would not want to listen. But a troubled *ka* wants peace and will listen to anything that may bring that peace."

I look up at her. "What do you mean?"

"Perhaps the time has come for us to find out why Ya wanted you raised as the grandson of Ramesses. But I am not comfortable talking to you where Kakemour or someone else might come in. Come to my apartment in the Women's Palace this afternoon during the time when Ramesses, Kakemour, and Intef always listen to petitions."

Almah was right. Something is going on. Mother knows what it is and thinks I can do something. I am excited but also frightened. What if I cannot live up to her expectations? What if she thinks I am capable of more than I am? What if Ya expects too much of me?

As I go down the broad staircase to make my usual morning appearance in the throne room, I am nervous. However, no one is whispering conspiratorially and neither does anyone pay attention to me. The scribes and priests greet me without a second glance. Grandfather, Intef, and Kakemour are going over the list of those who want audiences with the pharaoh this afternoon.

I used to sit next to Grandfather and listen to the

problems people brought for him to solve. Sometimes he would lean toward me, instead of Intef on his right, and ask what I thought he should do. I would tell him and, to my surprise, sometimes he agreed and would do the opposite of what he had planned.

Once a woman, the wife of a priest, had a child that was not the priest's. The woman claimed the child was a gift of the gods. The priest said the child belonged to another man. Grandfather believed the priest. Then, more out of fun than any sense that I might have something to say, he asked me what I thought. I said, "To believe the priest might undermine belief in the powers of the gods. If belief in the gods' powers is weakened, might that not affect yours?"

He looked at me sharply with those small piercing eyes of his. Then he turned to Kakemour. "And what does the next *tjat* think?"

"I would ask Mosis what would happen if many women suddenly had children by the gods? Would that not undermine *maat*?"

"Excellent question," Ramesses affirmed. "Mosis?"

"If it does, maybe the gods are not happy with the men."

Ramesses laughed loudly. "With a mind that subtle, you could be a dangerous man to have for an enemy, Mosis."

I noticed that neither Kakemour nor Intef laughed.

During the past year I have become uncomfortable watching people's happiness being decided by one man— sometimes me. Grandfather says, "It is *maat* we serve,

Mosis. Divine order. Every decision must increase *maat* and decrease *isfet*, 'chaos and injustice.'"

How does he know what is *maat* and what is *isfet*? I asked him once to give me a list so I would know which is which.

"It is not always that clear," he said.

"So how do you know?"

"I just do."

I don't know if that was the real answer or he couldn't tell me. Maybe the knowledge is imparted to him each morning when the priests bathe him in water mixed with saltwort and shave his entire body with a golden razor, plucking any remaining hairs with golden tweezers. Maybe the knowledge is in the oil they rub over his body or in the sacrifice he offers to the gods while the priests sing prayers and read to him from the sacred literature. Or perhaps not.

I used to enjoy looking down at the people as they kiss the ground at our feet. Now I am uneasy. Perhaps it is because Grandfather seems to have stopped listening to the people when they come with their problems. Even I am beginning to feel that they all sound alike, and I have to remind myself that the *people* with the problems are not alike. But Grandfather interrupts people now and gives decisions though he has not heard everything they came to say. He didn't used to be that way.

Just as I gradually stopped going to Goshen, I gradually stayed away from hearing cases. Even though I still appear each morning to pay my respects to Grandfather, I am sorry now that I have not been around as much. If I had been, I might know what they are planning, if any-thing. All I can do is wait impatiently for the afternoon.

IT HAS BEEN THREE YEARS since I moved from the Women's Palace, and I have had no reason to return until now, since Mother is seldom here anymore. Whichever con-cubines Ramesses wants near him live in the palace with their children. All of them want to be named Great Royal Wife, but no one has borne that title since Nefertari. I would be surprised if anyone ever did again.

More than any other place, however, this is home. It is where I lived for the first twelve years of my life, minus the three months or so when I was silent in Goshen. As I walk in I gaze at the paintings on both sides of the hall-way and am pleased that the ibises and hawks are still on their eternal flight, that the catfish has not yet been killed by the spear aimed at its side, that the arrow in Ramesses's bow has not yet been launched at the lion to the right of his chariot. I can see myself running through the hallways chasing or being chased by whatever chil-dren of Ramesses were around at the time. It is good to be here, to remember that there was a time when I was happy, when I was who I appeared to be.

As I go up the staircase to the second floor and Mother's apartment, some of the servants recognize me and bow. I smile and greet them by name, pleased that I remember them, too. They still think that I am who I ap-pear to be. Why isn't that enough for me?

Mother is seated on a couch as I come in, and she watches me as I look around and remember.

"What are you thinking?" she wants to know.

"Kittens should not become cats. I was happier when I was a kitten here."

Mother smiles wistfully. "Come. Sit. Perhaps the time has come when you can find happiness in being a cat."

I sit down, wishing she would tell me stories about when I was a child here. But she is even more serious than normal and begins talking immediately.

"As you know, next year will be Ramesses's thirtieth year as Pharaoh. Naturally, he wants to make it a year people will remember for a long time. But all is not going well. The Temple to Amon-Re being built in Pi-Ramesses was supposed to have been finished before the harvest. It will not be finished by this time next year unless something is done. Now that the harvest is almost over, Ramesses has decided to send soldiers into Goshen and force every Habiru—women, children, and old people—to work on the temple. That is the only way it can be finished in time."

"What?" I exclaim in disbelief. "That is not like Grandfather. He has always treated the Habiru like any other workers—Khemetian, Nubian, Midianite, or whomever. Is he also going to force their women, children, and old people to work on the temple?"

"No. Just the Habiru."

"This is a kind of slavery!" I exclaim.

"Yocheved says they have always been slaves. Only now it seems Ramesses is going to make them feel it. But I am not sure this was his idea. Asetnefret is eager to have the new temple finished because she wants to be married in it. Ramesses is going to make her Great Royal Wife."

"Asetnefret?" The name is familiar, but I can't place it.

"She was Second Royal Wife. After Mother died, Asetnefret disappeared. Quite frankly, I hoped Ramesses had had her killed. Unfortunately, that is not the case. She has been living at the Harem Palace in the Land of the Lakes, where he sent her after Mother died. She blames Almah because if Almah had not looked so much like Nefertari, Father would have made Asetnefret Great Royal Wife many years ago. He saw her on one of his visits a few years ago and, over time, she has managed to win his favor again. Even though Ramesses has more than thirty concubines and eighty children, he is lonely."

I remember now. Asetnefret hates Habiru. "How do you know all this, Mother?"

"I was sitting in the garden yesterday and Kakemour saw me. In the course of talking, he told me."

"How . . . how did he seem? I mean, was he pleased about Ramesses's decision?"

"He wasn't displeased," she responds after thinking about it. "But that's not important. The reason I have told you all this is because I think this is why Ya wanted you raised as the pharaoh's grandson."

"What do you mean?" I am hoping she doesn't think I can stop what is going to happen. "What . . . what can I do?" I ask her, my voice shaking.

"I don't know, but you must do something. How could you live with yourself if you didn't?"

I look at this woman I have always called Mother, though I have always known I did not enter this world through her body. For the first time, I see her as a woman apart—Meryetamun, daughter of Pharaoh, who has become Batya, daughter of God. She changed my life by bringing me to grow up in this palace, but I understand, also for the first time, that her life has been changed even more profoundly. If she had known what was going to happen, would she have picked that baby up out of the basket? I think she would have. The question is, if I had known what was going to happen, would I have let her?

I don't think so. What is she asking of me? Does she want me to tell Grandfather not to do what he is about to do? I may be his grandson, so to speak, but he is a god. Whether I believe that is not important. He believes it, and so does everyone else. There is nothing I can do, and I wish Mother would not act as if there were.

"Mother?"

"Yes."

"What are you going to do?"

"I think I will let my hair grow," she says simply. "I have tried to live in two worlds, but if Ramesses does this, then I choose to be Habiru. I would rather be with those who suffer than with those who cause suffering."

I am shocked and do not know what to say except no, Mother. Don't. If she chooses, it means I, too, will have to choose and I don't want to.

Mother looks around the room. "I have no place here anymore. I have not had a place here for three years now, since you moved to the main palace. Now that you are grown, I have nothing to do. I have no reason to remain here. In Goshen it is different."

"What's different?"

"I am the daughter Yocheved wanted Almah to be and the big sister Miryam wanted. And I no longer believe Taweret gave you to me. I am ashamed that I could ever have believed in a goddess with the body of a hippo and the head of a lion."

"And Almah thinks it is ridiculous to believe in a god you cannot touch or see."

"What do you believe, Mosis?"

I shake my head. "That is what Almah asked me. Abba, too."

"And what did you say?"

"I asked Almah a question. And perhaps I will ask it of you."

"What is it?"

"Will you love me if I want to serve Taweret, Hathor, Amon-Re, and all the others?"

She pauses for a long time, almost too long, I think, but then she says, finally, "It would not be easy, but yes— yes, I would. Mosis? Is that what you want to do, serve the gods of Egypt?"

I shake my head. "I don't know, Mother."

She smiles weakly. "I'm glad."

Chapter Four

AYS PASS. Nothing happens. Then, one morning as I walk into the throne room, all heads turn toward the door and everyone is suddenly silent and still. There are no smiles and nods of recognition. No one even bothers to greet me. Though I have often felt like a stranger here among these men, this is the first time I feel unwelcome and unwanted.

Normally I would walk across this huge room to where Grandfather sits in his throne chair, but he is not there this morning. Only Intef, who comes rapidly toward me and puts his arm around my shoulders. My body stiffens. He has never touched me and I do not think I want the feel of his touch now, but I do nothing to dislodge his arm.

"The pharaoh thinks it would be better if you did not come to the throne room for a while, or be seen about too much," he says quietly, turning me away from the room and starting to walk me back toward the door. "It has been necessary to force the Habiru to work on the new temple so it will be ready in time for the pharaoh's marriage to Asetnefret. Although the pharaoh has no doubts about your loyalty, there may be others here at court who wonder if you would be able to give your full support. Rather than risk any confrontations, the pharaoh thinks it wiser if you are not seen about for a while."

Intef has walked me rapidly into the hallway, and before I can say anything, he has turned and gone back inside. My face is burning with the heat of shame. Why didn't Grandfather tell me himself? Why did he wait until I came to see him? Why didn't he send someone to my suite this morning—or come himself? And where is Kakemour? He could have come and told me. But no! I am left to stand here while people hurry in and out of the throne room. Yesterday they greeted me: "In peace! In peace, Mosis, grandson of the pharaoh!" Today they walk past me as if I do not exist. Today I feel as if the very walls and floors were thinking *Mosis the Habiru!*

Tears are running down my face, but I do not care who sees. They may look like tears of hurt and sorrow—and I suppose several of them are—but most are tears of rage! But I do not know if I am angry at all those who knew me yesterday and will not speak with me today, angry at Grandfather for being afraid to tell me himself, or angry at myself for having played the game of Pharaoh's grandson. I am such a fool! Such a fool in my gold bracelets and perfumed wig and oiled body!

I run down the hall to the stairway leading up to the living quarters on the third floor, where I burst into

Almah's suite without knocking. The main room is empty and I am about to hurry out, when I see her standing on the balcony.

"Almah!"

She does not turn around. I go and stand beside her as my gaze follows hers. We are high enough here to see to the river, and there, on the Avenue of the Pharaoh, I see them, thousands of them—Habiru men, women, children, old people—walking toward Pi-Ramesses, soldiers standing almost shoulder to shoulder on each side.

I look at her and am surprised to see tears flowing down her face. Without a word we fall into each other's arms and hold each other tightly. Eventually we separate and go inside and sit in our usual positions on the couch. When we finally speak, it is in Habiru.

"I suppose, deep down, I was hoping Ramesses would change his mind," she says sadly. "I honestly didn't believe he would do this, not even after you told me what Batya said."

"Neither did I."

"Even so, as close as we are—or as close as I assumed we were—I would have thought he would have told me."

"He didn't say anything to you?" I exclaim incredulously.

"No. He didn't say anything to you?"

"When I went to the throne room a while ago, I was met with the silence of the dead. Intef told me not to come there anymore, or be seen around the palace, because they don't think I fully support what the pharaoh is doing."

"In other words, you are suspected of being disloyal, a traitor."

I nod, angry tears pooling in my eyes again.

"No one has told me anything. I didn't know a thing until I stepped out on the balcony this morning and saw the soldiers and the people. I couldn't believe my eyes. I almost didn't do the morning ritual today, but I knew that would make me look suspicious. And the goddess might not like it. When I got to the temple, I noticed the other priests and priestesses looking at me, trying to see if I knew, but I acted as if everything were normal. And when I went to see Ramesses, he was nowhere to be found."

"I think he is so ashamed that he doesn't know what to say to either of us."

"That is probably true," she agrees. "All of this was Asctnefret's idea. I know it!"

"How can you be sure?"

She sighs. "I probably shouldn't tell you this, but I think you need to know. When I was on my way from the temple to the palace this morning, I saw Kakemour. I was surprised because he is not usually out so early. But there he was, wearing his soldier's kilt and carrying a sword. 'Off to kill more Habiru babies?' I asked."

"You didn't?" I put in, incredulous and proud of my sister.

"I did."

"What did he say?"

"He turned red but more from anger than embarrassment, I think. But when he spoke...Well, for the first time in my life, I was afraid. He said, 'A piece of advice,

Priestess. I would be careful not to repeat such a comment. Habiru sympathizers will be thrown into prison. Even those who speak Khemetian as if they really are.' He was not hostile. Just matter-of-fact. That is what made it so frightening. Then he went on to tell me that at the same time the pharaoh marries Asetnefret, he, Kakemour, will be married to the youngest daughter of the pharaoh and Asetnefret. 'My interest in seeing the temple completed on time is a personal one, which is why I have been put in charge of seeing that it happens.'"

I don't understand. How could Kakemour, who is like a brother to me, marry the daughter of a woman who he knows hates Habiru? How could he do that? I loved him more than the brother of my blood.

"I don't understand," I say. "I don't understand how Grandfather and Kakemour could love us and yet do this. Did they love us in spite of our being born Habiru? Or were they able to love us only by pretending that we were not born Habiru?"

She shakes her head. "I don't think it's either. I think they always saw us as Meryetamun and Mosis. Two individuals. When they started plotting to put the Habiru into slavery, then they remembered that we are not only Meryetamun and Mosis, and suddenly their love for us is very confusing."

"I don't want to live like this anymore, Almah. I'm tired of thinking about who I am and what my place is. I keep thinking about going to Goshen. You know, it doesn't matter how they look at me or what they think about me there. They have to take me in because I, too, am a descendant of Avraham and Sarah, Yitzchak and Rivka, Yaakov, Rachel, and Leah. And I am the son of Amram and Yocheved."

I stop my pacing and look at her, but she is staring into her lap. The shadows of loneliness are deep in her face. I go to her and put my arms around her. "Almah? Come with me? Go back to Goshen with me? It might be hard at first, but we could make it work. We could! I know we could!" I would leave all this right now if Almah would come with me!

She disengages herself gently from my arms, and takes my face in the palms of her hands and looks at me. "The thought of losing you fills me with more fear than I know how to contain, Mosis. If marriage is two feelings becoming one feeling, then I am more married to you than I could be to any man. A woman is never truly married until her husband takes her away emotionally from her father and her brothers. It is easy to move her into another house, but feelings weigh more than a chair and no man could ever take you away from me."

Her hands drop from my face and I break into a smile. "Then it's settled!" I exclaim, getting up from the couch. "We will return to Goshen."

"No," she says immediately. "It is only because I love you so much that I can let you go. For you there is no other choice. You have no life here. I would have no life there."

"There would be something you could do," I plead.

"I belong to the goddess, Mosis. If I am going to pray to a god, and I must pray, then I'd rather it be a woman. Ya does not know how to receive my nakedness."

"Have you ever danced naked before Ya? How do you know? Maybe he's just waiting for a woman to dance naked for him." I know I am being ridiculous, but I will say anything, anything I can think of to convince her to come with me.

"Even when I was little, I had trouble with Ya. Who was he? Where was he? I remember the very first time I came to Pi-Ramesses. I couldn't have been more than two or three, but I remember the statues of all the gods and goddesses, and I knew then that being born something doesn't mean that's what you are. I didn't know that in words, but when Abba started teaching me Khemetian, it was the first time I felt like words belonged to me. These were words my mouth liked the feel of. And every little thing he told me about Khemet made sense. Why would a woman worship a male god like Ya when she can worship females like Eset and Hathor? Women need to see things and touch them. Ima has only one god. Maybe that's how men see things—men and the women who agree with them—but to me, as a woman, the world is too big and too complex. How can one god take care of everything for everybody? Having many gods and goddesses makes more sense.

"I'm sorry, Mosis, but I can't go back to Goshen. I know who I am here, even though I hate what Ramesses and Kakemour are doing—even though my own life may be in danger now that Asetnefret has returned to power. But this is the life I chose. This is the life I want. What I chose for me is not what you should choose for you."

She stands up and hugs me tightly. "I have to go to the temple for my midmorning ritual bath."

"I don't want to go without you," I say, and start to cry.

"Shhhh," she says softly, putting a finger to my lips.

And she hurries from the room, but not before I see the tears brimming in her eyes as I break into loud sobbing.

Chapter Five

I DO NOT KNOW HOW LONG I stay in Almah's suite. I am afraid to leave because, if I do, I may never see it or her again. But I am also afraid to be here when she comes back. Finally, when my eyes dry, I hurry down the hallway, hoping not to see anyone. Yet the hallway is empty, as if no one wants to see me, either.

I don't know what to do. Grandfather wants me to stay in here, see no one, and be seen by no one until the temple is completed; but that will be months. And how do I know life will return to normal after that? What if he decides he wants the Habiru to build him *another* temple?

I told Almah that I wanted to live in Goshen, but I would not make a good slave. I have never worked a day in my life, or had someone order me around, telling me what to do and when to do it. I wouldn't know how to take orders, and I don't want to learn. I am fooling myself if I think I could live in Goshen.

So what am I supposed to do? I will not be a slave, and if I stay here I will be a prisoner, or worse—a person whose life has no meaning in anyone's eyes, not even my own.

I go over it again and again in my mind. There has to be another choice. But if there is, I can't find it. Finally I am tired of thinking and tired of being confused. I need to get out of here, get some air, feel the sun on my body. But where can I go? I can't sit in Grandfather's garden, something I would do normally. I could go into Pi-Ramesses, but I'm not sure that's a good idea. I didn't go out during harvesttime because I was afraid of what I would see. Things are no better now.

But maybe that is what I should do. Go and see for myself. Maybe I'll find out that being a slave isn't as bad as I think it is. Or maybe it'll be worse. Either way, I will know where I want to be. And if I know that, then I'll know *who* I want to be.

SOLDIERS LINE THE Avenue of the Pharaoh on both sides, hands gripping their upraised spears as their eyes search the crowd for any untoward movement. The threat of death mingles with the smell of the lambs and cows being herded to the market. At the riverside I see Habiru men, women, and children unloading blocks of stone from barges, to load them on carts, which others pull toward the temple site in town.

The soldiers are outnumbered by the Habiru, who could attack the soldiers and take their spears and swords. But the Habiru do not seem to notice. They don't even look angry or resentful about what is happening to them.

133

I allow myself to be taken along with the crowds—Nubians, Lybians, Midianites, Syrians, Khemetians, and Habiru—toward where the new temple is being built. I do not like being jostled and bumped with almost every step I take, but I act as if I do not notice.

Finally I arrive at the temple building site. There is no doubt Ramesses will be remembered as the greatest builder in history. When I was small I remember being impressed by the temples—the scenes carved into the walls, the height of the columns. Today it does not make sense, especially when I think that I am supposed to be one of those men pulling that huge block of stone up the ramp. What would my life mean if this is all it was? Ramesses will be remembered throughout time, but his muscles will not ache from having moved even one stone. While all these whose muscles cry out for rest will be as nameless as grains of sand.

"Well, what a surprise!"

I recognize the voice and turn to see Kakemour, a big smile on his face, walking toward me down the broad temple steps. "So, what brings you into Pi-Ramesses?"

Despite myself I am glad to see him. His and Almah's faces have been more constant in my life than any others. It was easier to believe bad things about him when I couldn't see his smile. Seeing him now I am ashamed that I could have had a negative thought about him. I shrug. "Get away. Get outside."

He nods sympathetically. "Yes. I know. I am sorry it has to be that way for a while." He is holding a whip idly by his side.

"Why?" I want to know. "What is going on? One day everything normal. The next, I am not trusted."

Kakemour's face turns red. "We can't be too careful. Believe me. I argued with the queen—well, the soon-to-be queen. I told her you had lived in the palace every day of your life, practically. She said it would be safer if you kept a low profile until the temple is finished. She said it would be understandable if you had feelings about the necessity of forcing the Habiru to work. She wanted to spare you both the sight of it as well as minimize any risk that you might do something foolish."

"Such as?"

"Well, it would be understandable if you wanted to do something to help your parents and siblings. I know you wouldn't incite the Habiru against the pharaoh, but Asetnefret doesn't like to take chances."

Me? Incite someone? So, that's what this is about. Even though I grew up in the palace and Khemetian is my first tongue and I look Khemetian, they think of me as Habiru. Mother was right! This is all the doing of Asetnefret. "Grandfather?" I ask hesitantly, wanting to know what he said.

Kakemour looks away, as if something a worker is doing has caught his eye, but he doesn't want to look at me, doesn't want to see me looking at him.

"He thought it was a good idea. It's not that he doesn't trust you. No, no. Nothing like that. But you know the inner workings of the palace, where the horses and chariots are kept, the routines of the guards, all of which is valuable information. What if some Habiru hotheads

135

decide to organize a rebellion? They could kidnap you, torture you, and you would have no choice but to tell them everything you know about palace life. I'm sure that no one will mind your being here today, but if you come into the city on too many more days, that might arouse suspicion."

Anger rises in me slowly like the river when the floods are beginning. They do not trust either of us. They have never accepted me as one of them. I am tolerated but I do not belong.

Kakemour tries to smile. "What are you worrying about these things for? It is not for the likes of men like you and me to get too involved in such heavy matters."

He is trying to appease me, but he insults my intelligence. He is the future *tjat* and son-in-law to the pharaoh. This is precisely the kind of thing he must be involved in. When Kakemour goes to put his arm around me as if we are going for a chariot ride or to take a boat onto the river and hunt ducks, I know he is not taking me seriously and I brush his arm off. "I'm not a child! Talk to me like an adult!"

The smile leaves his face so suddenly I wonder if it was really there. "Very well. You want to know the truth. No one wants to hurt your feelings. I don't, either, but you're right. You're not a child any longer. You deserve the truth."

There is a hardness in the center of his eyes that I have never seen. Or maybe I simply never noticed.

"I have always wondered whose side you would be on," he says calmly. "When you and your sister first came to live here, I tried to explain to her, once, why Khemetians do not trust Habiru, can never trust Habiru. Nothing has changed. Queen Asetnefret is right. She was right fifteen years ago when Meryetamun took leave of her senses and brought you here. And if Queen Nefertari had not died when she did, Queen Asetnefret would have had her way."

I look at him sharply and he stops. I have to ask him. I have to know. "That night. Fifteen years ago. Would you have killed me?" I stop, but my eyes bore into his until he explodes in anger.

"How dare you ask me that! Do you not understand that nothing is more important than *maat*? But that is a concept no Habiru can grasp, not even you, who grew up with it. How can you trust a people who speak another language and worship another god? In an emergency— and this is an emergency—where does their loyalty lie? You grew up in the pharaoh's palace as his grandson, but your *ka* is still Habiru."

"No!" I shout back. "I am loyal to Ramesses. But this"—and my arms fling out to embrace the Habiru working—"no!"

Kakemour shakes his head "No, Mosis! No! There is only one issue. Building this temple to the glory of Amon-Re and Pharaoh. Nothing else matters. But perhaps you do not believe that the sun rises each day only because of the pharaoh's rituals and prayers. Perhaps you do not really believe the pharaoh is a god who has taken on human form and there is nothing greater than his presence in our midst. Look around you, Mosis! Look at these people working here, people from all over the world. All of them pay homage to Pharaoh. Look, Mosis! Many of those working here are Khemetians! We did not have to send soldiers to get them to come work. Old and young! When they heard that more workers were needed to complete the temple on time, they volunteered— women, children, old people. For them it is an honor to work here. 'Tell me what I can do!' they wanted to know. Only the Habiru had to be forced. Yet the pharaoh permits the Habiru to live on the richest land in all Khemet. But when the pharaoh needs them for something, not only do they not come voluntarily, when they are forced to come, they act like they are being marched to their deaths. You think I am cruel. I think the Habiru are ungrateful. I would not want to have the same opinion of you."

I have never seen him so angry. The short whip is trembling in his hand as if his emotions are more than his body can contain. With a shock I realize that he wants to hit me and would do so if he were sure Grandfather would not be angry.

But why? Why is he so angry that he would whip me if he could? Because he thinks I am ungrateful? But ungrateful for what? I did not ask to be raised in the pharaoh's palace. Yes, I am glad that Ya or Taweret decided that I would, but has Kakemour been merely doing me a favor all these years? Maybe that is it. Maybe I was never his little brother as much as I was a duty he had to carry out as future tjat. Maybe Grandfather told him to be like a brother to me. Otherwise he would not have done it.

"So, you don't have anything to say, Mosis?"

The thing that would satisfy me now would be to snatch the whip from his hand and slash him across the face. And that would not be good, so I shake my head and back away, stumbling against someone who pushes me off him and into the crowd.

All day I let the throngs of people push me in this direction and that, as if I am walking in my sleep. Once, I find myself by a ship being unloaded, and the next time, I am surprised to find myself wandering through the marketplace.

Morning becomes afternoon and I am more confused than ever. Coming out was supposed to help me know what to do. But things are worse. Knowing now how they really think of me, I can't live in the palace. But I cannot go to Goshen and become a slave.

I do not recognize that I have wandered full circle back to the new temple until I hear Kakemour call my name. "Mosis!"

At the mere sound of his voice anger surges back into me. I turn around but don't see him.

"Here!"

I see an arm waving to me from the shadows beneath the obelisks at the entrance of the temple. I go up the broad steps and across the porch. I can see now that he is holding someone by the arm, but I cannot tell who it is. As I get closer, I recognize who it is and I want to run away.

Like Abba he has a full beard, only his is night black. I wonder if I would look like him if I grew a beard. I hope he does not recognize me. Why would he? He always avoided me as if I were a crocodile sunning in the middle of the road. Unlike Abba, whose skill is his intelligence, Aharon's hands have an intelligence of their own in the way they can paint a wall and make the figures on them look alive, or carve a ram, a bull, or a calf from the hardest stone and make them so real you are disappointed they are not.

"I've been looking for you," Kakemour says. His lips are smiling, but his eyes are thin with malice.

I try not to look at Aharon. I do not want to know if he knows who I am. But Kakemour makes sure he does.

"It didn't take me long to find your brother. He is known to everyone, as well he should be. He is very talented. Now you will probably think that what I am about to do is cruel. But if you stop and think about it, if you remember all you learned about *maat* from the priests, you would understand that as the son of the *tjat*, as the future *tjat*, as the future son-in-law of the queen and the pharaoh, it is my obligation to be sure that *isfet* is uprooted no matter where it appears."

I know what he is going to ask me to do even before he says it.

"We need to be sure whose side the so-called grandson of the pharaoh is on. Here. Take my whip and use it on your brother. I don't expect you to really hurt him. I'm not a cruel man. I'm not asking you to draw blood. Hit him with the whip. Just once. That's all. It would make such a difference if tonight, at dinner, I could tell Queen Asetnefret that I saw you whip your brother."

Aharon looks at me, but his eyes are expressionless. It is as if he does not know who I am, or maybe worse, does not care that I am his brother. Whatever those eyes are saying, it is clear that they are not afraid and they are not pleading.

Kakemour holds out the short whip he was carrying this morning. Instinctively I take it and am immediately ashamed. What am I doing? I can't strike my own brother. But what would it matter in the long run? I could just touch him lightly with the leather thongs. Aharon would understand. He's practical. And I could make it up to him. Have food sent from the palace for his meal every day, or see that he gets an extra ration of beer. If I don't hit him, I am a traitor to *maat*. Who knows what will happen to me?

I tighten my grip on the whip's smooth wood handle. I imagine drawing back my arm and bringing it down lightly, and then harder and harder. I can almost hear the sound of the leather against bare flesh, can almost see the welts rising on the skin, almost smell the blood trickling through the lacerated flesh.

Then I see the smirk on Kakemour's face and I know! I know what the rest of my life will be like if I whip Aharon. Kakemour will never let me forget I did it. He will never stop asking me to prove my loyalty to the pharaoh. This will not be the end of his testing me but the beginning of something that will never end. Suddenly I remember the first time I saw Almah dance and how the pharaoh stood and applauded her and Kakemour did not. He did not smile even. Suddenly I know, without a doubt, that one day Kakemour will ask me to prove my loyalty by doing something to Almah. He does not know this yet, but when Asetnefret or his new bride see how close the pharaoh and Almah are, they will ask him to do something about "that Habiru priestess" and he will come to me. If I strike my brother now, I will strike my sister then. Or worse.

My arm draws back and before Kakemour realizes what is happening, I am whipping him across the face as hard as I can. His grip on Aharon loosens as he screams in pain and raises his hands to his bleeding face and falls to the ground.

I draw back my arm to strike him again and again, but Aharon knocks the whip from my hand and pushes me away.

"You fool! Now you've made things worse, much worse. Who knows what that Khemetian will do now? He could have us killed, all of us—Ima, Abba, Miryam, and me. And why? All because you were too scared to graze my skin with that whip when he as much as told you that all you had to do was pretend you were whipping me."

Aharon doesn't understand. But he is also right. I have put my family's life in jeopardy.

"Get out of here," he tells me. "I'll stay and help this Khemetian get to a physician. Maybe that will keep him from bringing soldiers to kill us."

I hurry from the temple. I am frightened, yet strangely at peace, too. For the first time in my life, I have done something.

Chapter Six

I HAVE NO CHOICE. I must go to Goshen. I don't dare return to the palace, but I have to tell Almah what has happened. And Mother. But before I do that I want to go back and be sure that Aharon, Abba, Ima, and Miryam are safe. And to tell them that I am coming. I am coming... home.

I wander aimlessly, down the side streets near the temple, anxiously waiting for the workday to end and everyone to start for home. I am nervous, even a little frightened but also excited.

Finally the day is ending and people are beginning to leave. When I make my way back to the temple, the Khemetian workers are going slowly up the Street of the Queen to the Workers' Village on the other side of the river.

I look around for Aharon but don't see him. I want to run after the workers and ask them if anything happened this afternoon, if soldiers came and took some Habiru away, but I do not want to draw attention to myself. I can just hope everyone is all right.

I must get back to the palace to see Almah and Mother. Kakemour is already there by now and has told Intef what happened. Soldiers are probably on their way to look for me, and the palace guards will be on the lookout. It will be best if I cross over the Hapi and follow the Avenue of the Crocodiles. More than once I have helped Kakemour get back to the palace that way, stumbling across the sand after the street ends, and sneaking in the back way past the stables and the slaughtering pens.

As I fall in quietly with the Khemetian workers walking toward the village, no one notices as it is not unusual for young noblemen to cross over to their side. The crowds thin quickly as workers disappear down the many side streets to their houses. I continue parallel to the river on the Avenue of the Crocodiles, walking casually as if I have no particular destination in mind but with enough purpose that I appear to know where I am going.

The sun is going down behind me when, two streets ahead, I see a Khemetian nobleman coming out of a side street. I step back quickly and press myself against a house, though when he looks my way, the sun is directly in his eyes. However, because the sun illuminates him, I can see him clearly. It is Kakemour! He turns and goes in the direction I am headed. I don't understand. What's he doing over here? Why isn't he at the palace telling everyone I am a traitor?

When I get to the street out of which he came, I look down it, wondering who could live here that he would have come to see. And then I see the sign: PHYSICIAN. I still don't understand. Why would Kakemour come here to see a doctor when he could be tended to by the Physician to the Pharaoh? Then it comes to me! He doesn't want anyone to know that I beat him with his own whip.

He is going to sneak back into the palace the same way I am planning to. The doctor probably gave him some salves to put on the cuts, and by tomorrow morning his face will not look as bad as it probably does now and he will have thought of some story to tell Intef and no one will ever know what really happened. But he will, which means that one day soon, he will take his revenge on Aharon, Abba, Ima, or Miryam. No. No, he won't. He will find a way to hurt Almah because that will hurt me the most.

I follow him at a safe distance so that if he should happen to look back he would not recognize me. But he only looks straight ahead. As the sun goes lower I know what I have to do. The simple logic of it is almost a relief.

I search the pavement until I find what I am looking for and my hand curls around the large stone. It fits perfectly and grows warm, as if drawing power from deep within me.

We have left the avenue behind and there is now only sand. One is as likely to stumble across an alligator or snake as someone who has fallen asleep from drinking too much palm wine. No one lives here, and the sandy soil makes it impossible to grow anything.

I move quickly and quietly to close the distance between us. Only when I am almost on him does he hear something or sense my presence and turn around. Recognition comes into his eyes, and as he opens his mouth to say my name, I slam the stone into the side of his head. He drops to the ground like a goose knocked from the sky by a throwing stick. I am about to hit him again when I see that he has not moved.

I bend over to hear if he is breathing. He doesn't seem to be. Taking his wrist, I feel for his pulse. There is none. His eyes are closed, and my fingers feel clumsy as I peel back his eyelid. There is no life in the eye that stares back. He is dead. Kakemour is dead!

I am breathing so heavily that the sound is almost deafening in my ears. My stomach starts cramping, and before I know it I am bending over his body, retching and vomiting so violently I fear I will see my innards pour from my mouth. Eventually, nothing is left to come up. I wipe my mouth with the back of my hand, but the taste of my own filth remains on my tongue and in my throat.

Frantic, I look around but see no one. What am I going to do? I have to bury the body. Taking his ankles, I drag him away from the river and start digging with my hands but the sand keeps sliding back into the hole. Finally, in frustration I throw as much sand over his body as I can and hurry away without looking back.

No one sees me as I slip into the palace grounds and to my suite. I need to sleep. That is all I want to do—go to bed and sleep and wake up to learn that this day was an awful nightmare and tonight Kakemour will take me to a banquet and I will drink palm wine and be very happy.

But when I close my eyes, I see Kakemour's head turning, his eyes meeting mine, his lips beginning to form my name, and after that I remember little. Except that he is dead. Murdered. By me.

The gray of morning comes. I have not slept. I must tell someone. I get up and go to the Women's Palace, hoping Mother has not left for Goshen. I ease myself into her room, and just as she awoke when I was an infant if I so much as turned my head, she awakes now.

"Mosis?"

I go to her, and as I put my arms around her, I start crying as I did not do even as a child. She does not ask me what's wrong but holds me tightly.

Finally my crying slows, then quiets, and I tell her. "I killed Kakemour," I say in a hollow voice. I want to explain but do not know what I would say.

She gasps and I start sobbing again and she hugs me closer, rocking me back and forth, back and forth. This must have been what it was like to be a baby in her arms, and how I wish I could be that again. But I can't. Eventually my sobbing diminishes to an occasional sniffle, and as I watch the light grow brighter and spread across the ceiling and then down the walls, a tear drops onto my hand. Pulling back I see tears covering her face. She utters no sound, but her face is as broken as a bowl that has been knocked off a table. I do not know if she is crying for him or me or because nothing will ever be the same again.

"Sorry," I whisper. "I'm sorry."

She nods, wiping the tears from her face. "I never told you that Kakemour wanted to marry me once."

"Oh, Mother! I . . . I—"

"It's all right. We were not meant for each other. But it is hard to think of him as dead and by the hand of my son. What happened?"

I shake my head. I don't want to talk about it. I don't want to think about it. "I'm sorry," I say again, as if those simple words can undo what cannot be undone.

"I know. Well, we have to do something."

"What?"

"I don't know. Have you told Almah?"

"No."

"We must. I'll see if I can find her. She'll know what to do."

Mother leaves the room, and in a little while she is back.

"Almah is coming."

As we wait in silence, I go over in my mind what happened yesterday, how what was supposed to be a walk into Pi-Ramesses turned into a murder. I know it made sense then. Why doesn't it make sense now? At least sense enough that I could make Mother and Almah understand. Even if I were to tell them that I thought he was going to hurt Almah in some way, did I have to kill him? Then I wonder.

Was it him I was killing, or was it something in myself I wanted dead—my self-loathing for ever thinking of him as my brother, for believing that I mattered to him, my self-hatred for not knowing who I really am. If only I had not gone to Pi-Ramesses yesterday and instead had gone to Goshen and said, *This is my home.* If only.

Almah enters and I tell her.

"Why, Mosis? Why?" she asks, fear and shock flooding her eyes.

I can't tell her. I can't let her see that the person she loves so much is not as wonderful as she thinks.

She turns away to stare at the wall, and I wonder what memories this room holds for her, because she lived here, too, for a little while. Is she remembering all the way back to that first day when she came here with Ima and me? Is she, too, wondering how I got from that day to this?

"What shall we do?" Mother asks softly, breaking the silence.

Almah turns and her eyes catch mine, but I quickly look down at my hands in my lap. "Mosis?"

My head raises involuntarily, and this time her eyes hold me.

"The choice is yours. You can stay here, but that will mean either confessing to Kakemour's murder or living a lie for the rest of your life."

I shake my head. I cannot do either. If I confess, I will probably be killed. And I am not a good liar. The truth would protrude from my face like the snake's head on the pharaoh's headdress. "No. I can't do either."

"Then, you must go to Goshen."

I nod. "I know. Then what? Become a slave?"

"No. I'll think of something."

"Come to Goshen with me?" I ask, knowing the answer but needing to ask the question.

She shakes her head. "I can't. You know that. I'll be all right. Don't worry. Now you must go back to your suite quickly, before too many are about. Late this afternoon you and Batya are to make your way to Ima and Abba's house. Try to sneak out without being seen. I will meet you there after sunset. But do not tell anyone I am coming. If I cannot make it tonight, I will be there as soon as I can. By then I will have figured out what to do next."

WHEN MOTHER AND I arrive in Goshen, everyone is surprised and happy to see me. But Abba and Ima are also puzzled by my visit. Though they do not say anything, I can tell from the way they look at me that they know something is wrong, especially since I am not wearing jewelry or makeup. I am glad they do not ask, but not as glad as I am that Aharon gives me a big hug.

"My brother has returned," he says with a smile. "Forgive me for what I said to you yesterday," he whispers in my ear, holding me close. "I am sorry to say that I was frightened by what you did. Frightened, surprised, and finally, excited. I did not know you cared so much about us. Is that why you are here? Has the Khemetian you whipped threatened you? I was concerned because when we went to work this morning, he was not there."

"What happened after I left? Did you take him to a doctor?"

"I tried to help him, but he told me to get away from him and staggered inside the temple, and that is the last I saw of him."

Ima chatters as she makes supper. I have never heard her talk so much. It does not matter that she talks about nothing. She is happy that I have come home. I wonder how happy she will be when she finds out why.

We eat. Night comes. We sit in the dim light of a lamp. The excitement of my being there has quieted. Now is the time for explanations, but neither Abba nor Ima will ask. They know we are waiting, but for whom or what is not clear until the door opens.

Ima gasps as Almah walks in, but before she can say anything, Almah has crossed the room and is hugging her, tears flowing down her face. Ima's arms make their way around the body of her daughter, and there are tears in her eyes. When they release each other, Almah hugs Aharon, Miryam, and finally, Abba.

There is much sniffling and wiping of eyes, and small bursts of nervous laughter from Almah and Ima. Finally Almah sits on the floor, Ima on one side of her, Mother on the other. I look at them, my three mothers, together in the same room, side by side.

"Have you told them?" Almah asks me.

I shake my head, not wanting to remember why I am here.

"What's the matter?" Ima wants to know.

"Mosis killed the son of the *tjat*, the man who was going to marry one of the daughters of Asetnefret and himself be *tjat* one day," Almah says matter-of-factly.

"What?" Abba asks, shocked.

"He killed a Khemetian," Ima says with pleasure in her voice. "An important Khemetian, it sounds like."

"Why, Mosis?" Abba asks in a pained voice.

"The Khemetians offend Ya. That's reason enough," Ima interjects.

"No, it isn't," Almah answers calmly, "but there isn't time for this. Mosis, Kakemour's body was found this afternoon. Because no one has seen you since yesterday, Ramesses wonders if you were killed also. Intef, however, wonders if you aren't the killer and have come here to hide. Ramesses is sending soldiers in the morning to look for you."

"What shall I do? No basket big enough this time."

Almah smiles sadly. "No. There isn't. There is no place in Khemet where you would not be found. You have to go."

I look at her, shock, disbelief, and panic coming into my eyes with such rapidity that I am ashamed. "What?"

"You cannot stay in Goshen and you cannot stay in Khemet. If you want to live." I hear a catch in Almah's voice as she says the last.

"I don't believe this," I manage to say. I look around at them—Abba, Ima, Mother, Aharon, Miryam, and Almah—my eyes pleading. They look back, Ima and Mother with tears in their eyes, but no one's eyes answer my plea.

"Why?" I say angrily. "No one saw."

"I'm not sure," Almah says. "Just because you saw no one doesn't mean you weren't seen. As I was leaving the palace tonight, I was stopped by a servant. He was not Habiru, but he spoke Habiru. He told me that he overheard two Habiru saying they had seen the Habiru who dresses like a Khemetian following someone as they left the temple yesterday."

"That's a lie!"

"Mosis!" It is Abba. "I am ashamed of you. Almah is risking her life by being here tonight."

I drop my head and then look up. "Forgive me," I say to Almah. "I . . . I am afraid. I don't know where to go. And what will I do once I get somewhere? I hadn't planned on any of this."

"No, but Ya did," Ima interjects. "All these years I have told myself that Ya took you to live among idol-aters because he had great plans for you. Now I under-stand. What you have done, my son, is good! You killed a Khemetian! You could do that only because you have known something we don't. Freedom! You know what it feels like to be free! Free! Growing up as the pharaoh's grandson, you have breathed nothing but freedom. Since the death of Yosef, no Habiru has been free— until you. You must go and come back and teach us all to be free."

I nod my head slowly, though right now I do not feel free.

Almah gets up from the floor. "I'm sorry I have to go so soon," she says, hugging Ima again, then everyone else. "But it is time for Mosis to leave."

"What . . . what is your plan, Almah?"

Everyone looks at Ima. It is the first time in my life I have heard that name pass her lips. Almah is startled, too, and she blinks her eyes rapidly to hold back the tears.

"It is better if you don't know, Ima. Then, when the soldiers come tomorrow and ask where Mosis is, you can say truthfully that you don't know."

Ima smiles and nods her agreement. There is nothing else to do but hug everyone, to look at them and try to impress their faces on my mind, as I will never see them again. Most difficult of all is leaving Mother. She is sobbing uncontrollably, and now it is my turn to hold her as if she were a baby. As I do so, I feel that everything will be all right. I don't know how. But it will.

"Come. We must hurry."

I wipe Mother's tears from her face with my hands and, giving her one last hug, follow Almah into the darkness.

Epilogue

I GET UP WHEN I SEE the blackness on the ceiling change to gray. I do not know how long I have been awake. Sometimes I wonder if I have slept at all since Mosis left. The emptiness inside me seems as deep and unending as the blackness of night. I understand now why Batya cried so much when Nefertari died. I did not know my body held so many tears.

I don't cry as much now as I did the first month. Then it was all through the night, every night. I do not cry as often now or for as long a period of time, but I feel raw inside, as if my heart were hanging from a tree.

It is light enough to see the dim outlines of the feathers on Eset's wings on the wall painting across from my bed. If I did not have the goddesses to serve, I would have died. No, that is not true. If not for the goddesses, I would have gone with him. I almost did that night. As we made our way out of Goshen, I began thinking that I would never see him again, that he would never again be waiting for me at the end of my day, that I would never sit and share silence with him. He will never know how close I came to saying, *I will come with you.*

But I couldn't, not when I thought about what the reaction would be when both Mosis and I could not be found. I was not sure how the pharaoh would respond when he realized Mosis was gone. But if we were both missing he would send soldiers as far as Syria to find us. My staying was Mosis's best protection.

I had to stay also because if I leave Khemet, my *ka* will die. This is where I have to be in order to be myself. No matter how much I miss Mosis, it would be far more awful to live with eternal longing for myself. And so I watched the darkness swallow him just as it swallows the sun each evening. But we have the pharaoh to make the sun return each morning. There is no one who can make Mosis return. Ima insists that Ya will send him back when Ya has made him ready. If Mosis were to come back, I think I would be convinced that Ya is more powerful than all the other gods.

I pour water into a bowl and wash my hands three times and then put water lightly on my face in order to make a separation between my night self and the me who is coming into being with the new day. Then I go out into the hallway.

The palace is completely still. My bare feet do not make a sound on the tiled floors as I make my way toward the stairs to the roof. As I pass the suite of rooms where Mosis lived, I try not to think that the daughter of Aset-nefret who was to have married Kakemour lives there now. I try not to think or remember much these days.

When I reach the roof, the eastern sky is tinged with dark blue. To the north, in Goshen, Abba and Aharon stand on a roof looking at the same sky. I hope that somewhere on the other side of the desert Mosis is also looking at this sky.

It has been almost six weeks since I made it seem that the mules had broken from their pen so Mosis could ride away on one into the desert. The servants spent much of the following morning trying to catch the mules, and in so doing, their footprints obliterated those of the one mule that carried weight on its back. Though I overheard speculation about how the mules got out, no one suspected the truth.

I sit down and, crossing my legs, I close my eyes and begin breathing deeply and slowly. I focus on the ingoing and outgoing of my breath, shedding my mind's desire to indulge in useless speculations about whether he is alive and where he might be. I have no other awareness than that of my breath, in which is my life and my *ka*. This is who I am, this breath, this life, this *ka*.

"In peace, my daughter."

Ramesses's voice startles me. I turn my head. He has not yet put on eye makeup or a wig, and his baldness gives him the appearance of even more strength than he normally has. He is wearing only a kilt, and I can see the stubble of hair on his legs, indicating that he has not been shaved yet.

"I did not mean to startle you," he continues.

"That's all right," I say, unable to hide the apprehension in my voice. Why is he here? It must be urgent because no one is permitted to see him without a wig on. Has he come to tell me that they have caught Mosis, or that his body was found in the desert? I start to get up, but he motions me to remain seated and comes to sit beside me.

"Relax. I knew I would find you here. I wanted to talk without other ears about. We have not talked, father to daughter and daughter to father, since the murder, and the disappearance of Mosis."

I am not sure I want to know what he is hinting at, but my face remains expressionless. Though I am with him each day, it is after he has dressed. Seeing him thus, I am surprised by the weariness in his eyes, at the shadow of age hovering over him.

He smiles. "After all these years I still look at you and see her. I don't know how I would have survived if I had not had you. I wanted to marry you, you know, and would have, but you never seemed interested. Did you know?"

I nod. "A woman knows when a man's desires are reaching for her, even when she is twelve."

"And how does that feel?"

"It depends. On the man. Sometimes it is flattering. Sometimes it is intrusive. And sometimes it is elevating."

"And how did my desire for you feel?"

"Elevating but intrusive," I respond simply. "I knew I was not her. If I had let you marry me, you would have been more aware of what had been taken from you, not what had been given."

"Perhaps, but you could have been Queen of Khemet.

Isn't that what every woman wants?" He says this last with a touch of sarcasm.

"I am a better daughter and priestess than wife, yours or any man's."

He nods. "Only when I saw that you desired no man, none except your brother, was I able to let you be."

The sky is white where the sun has risen. I should have begun my morning prayers already. However, it is not every day that the pharaoh wants to talk to you.

"You and your mother speak now?" he asks, after a long pause.

I am surprised, but little happens in Khemet that Ramesses does not know. "Yes. Yes, we do. I visit every week or so. We have agreed that she can talk to me about Ya, but I will not speak of Eset or Hathor to her."

He chuckles. "A wise decision, I would think."

"I don't mind. Mainly, though, we talk about how hard life is now. She wants to know why you have become cruel to the Habiru. Because everyone now works from sun to sun, they do not have time to tend their gardens, and the food you have provided for them is not enough. Women, children, and old people die every day from the hard work and from accidents. This is not like you."

He looks sharply at me and I wonder if I have crossed a boundary, but his face softens. "I should have made you *tjat*. You are not afraid of me. But you know the answer to your question. The Habiru disturb *maat*. They have been in Khemet for more than two hundred years, and yet, they still live as strangers among us. They keep to themselves. They will not eat with us. They will not socialize with us. They refuse to learn our language. This goes against the divine order. The hard labor I have imposed on them is the only way I can protect *maat*."

"You could let them go free."

"That would disturb *maat* most of all. It would seem like I was rewarding them for their defiance of the divine order. Let their Ya come and free them. I won't. And speaking of Ya, how is the daughter of god?"

There is a tinge of sarcasm in his voice, but I ignore it. "Batya is well. She is the daughter Ima always wanted."

"Don't you have a sister?"

"Miryam. She's a little odd. Like me. I am getting to know her. The other day she asked me what it feels like to dance."

"Does the daughter of god ever ask about me?"

"No. She is angry, and she is ashamed of what you are doing to the Habiru."

"And you?" he asks, looking at me with those eyes one cannot lie to.

"I am sorry to say that I understand. I believe in *maat*. But I don't like what you have done."

"I'm not sorry you feel that way. Asetnefret and Intef derive too much pleasure from what I am doing to the Habiru. I have none. I do what I do because I am the guardian of Khemet."

"I will tell Batya what you said."

"Thank you. Tell her, also, that I miss her."

Half of the sun's disk is above the horizon now, and

the clear sky seems to be inhaling the light. I am enjoying talking with Ramesses, but I also wish he would go so I could greet the day.

"I had a visitor a week or so ago," he says too casually. "A Syrian. It seems that he had just come from the land of Midian, where he stayed a few days with a priest named Yitro. Living in Yitro's house was a young man who spoke Khemetian."

My facial expression does not change, but my heart feels like it stops beating.

"What was odd, the traveler said, was that the young Khemetian was not a runaway servant or slave. He had the bearing of one from the nobility. I'm sure the traveler would have said more, but I showed no curiosity and he went on to talk about other things. But I sent my son Merenptah to investigate. He returned and confirmed what I thought was the case. Please tell your mother I regret that I cannot ease her physical burden, but perhaps it will lighten her *ka*—and yours—to know that Mosis is alive and well."

I cannot restrain myself, and I throw my arms around his neck and hug him tightly. "Thank you. Thank you." Although it is forbidden to touch the pharaoh, I have always been the exception, besides his wives and concubines, of course.

"Did Mosis kill Kakemour?"

That is like Ramesses, to ask what he really wants to know when you are feeling most tender toward him. I sit back. "Yes."

"Why?"

"I asked him that. He would not say at first, but finally, just . . . just before he left, he needed me to know. He was angry that you did not want him to leave the palace grounds until after the temple was finished, that you no longer trusted him."

"How did he know this?"

"That is what both Intef and Kakemour told him. It seems that Kakemour decided to test Mosis's loyalty to you by trying to make Mosis beat his brother, Aharon, with a whip. Instead Mosis used the whip on Kakemour. Mosis was afraid Kakemour would try to take his revenge on me, and to protect me, Mosis felt he had no choice but to murder Kakemour."

Ramesses is quiet for a long time. "It is too bad Mosis did not come and ask me."

"Why is that?" I ask, confused.

"I gave no orders for Mosis to be confined to the palace grounds."

"You didn't?" I am shocked.

"No. Do you really think I was afraid Mosis would foment rebellion among the Habiru? Mosis had my trust far more than he knew. I was not happy at the thought of Kakemour becoming *tjat* and my son-in-law. That was putting too much power at Asetnefret's disposal. I was going to make Mosis *tjat* after the wedding. I would not be surprised if Kakemour sensed my displeasure with him and tried to provoke Mosis, thus giving Kakemour an excuse to kill him. He underestimated Mosis's intelligence and courage, and now he is dead."

I am stunned. Mosis as *tjat*. It would not have worked. Perhaps Ya knew that Mosis had to leave Khemet, and the murder of Kakemour was the only way that could be arranged.

"And you? Did you help Mosis escape?"

I was not expecting this question, either. I want to tell him no. I have never done anything he would disapprove of—except that. But to lie would hurt him more than the truth. "Yes."

He nods. "When I heard that Kakemour had been murdered, I was shocked. We do not have murders in Khemet. Nothing disturbs *maat* so greatly as murder. Then I heard Mosis was missing, and I feared he had been murdered, too. But Intef and Asetnefret thought otherwise, especially because the mules so mysteriously broke out of their pen—and one has not yet been found. I knew then that they were right, though I did not tell them. I wanted to send soldiers after him and have him brought back so I could kill him myself. But I could not have done that. Have Mosis executed? I loved him more than many of my own sons. So, better that he not be caught. Then there is nothing I have to do. There is nothing I have to admit. I know where he is. I know he is well. That is enough.

"Incidentally, both Asetnefret and Intef were convinced you helped Mosis escape. I thought that was probably so, too. But when you appeared the morning after Kakemour's body was discovered and expressed your grief to Asetnefret and Intef, they did not know what to think. I saw the tension in your face, and I admire your being able to hold it all within—the murder, the loss of your brother, the need to help him escape, and above all, your loyalty to me, to the gods, to Khemet. As long as I live, Asetnefret will not harm you. And I expect to outlive her by many years." He laughs softly.

"Now I apologize. I have kept you from your morning prayers. I know the priests restrict you to the service of Eset and Hathor." He chuckles. "And well they should. If you were to start doing other rituals, they would be out of jobs. Though you are forbidden to sing the Hymn to Osiris, I have no doubt that you know it."

I smile. "Of course."

"You will sing it for me?"

I rise. The sun's disk is almost entirely above the horizon now. If I were alone I would remove my dress and stand naked to receive the new day and the new life it brings into my being. But I do not want to awaken desire in Ramesses. And then I think, no, I cannot let his presence alter the way I pray. Let his eyes and mind do what they will. This morning of all mornings my heart bursts with the need to thank the gods for keeping Mosis safe.

I remove my dress, and the sun covers my body with its soft warmth. I close my eyes and throw back my head until my face is parallel with the sky. Then slowly I raise my arms straight up from my body, and then lower them until they are even with my shoulders and draw them in front of my body, palms upraised, and I sing:

"Greetings to you, Osiris, Lord of eternity, King of the gods.
Your names are many; your forms are holy.
For you the waters are poured out.
For you the winds approach at evening.
The heights of heaven and the stars obey you.
He makes the mighty gates to open before him, Osiris,
Who is praised in the southern heaven
And adored in the northern heaven.
The never-setting stars are under his rule
And his abodes are the stars that never rest.
He has set his fear in all lands, and
Through their love for him,
They exalt his name above every other name.
All nations praise him and with one voice
Utter cries of joy. With his hand
He made this earth, and the water, air,
Vegetation, cattle, feathered fowl, fishes,
Creeping things, and beasts of all kinds.
He rises in the horizon. He lightens the darkness.
He floods the Two Lands with splendor in the early morning.
He is gracious in speech.
He is the favored one of the gods."

As the sound of the hymn dies, I open my eyes. Through my tears I see that the full disk of the sun rests on the edge of the world. Somewhere in the land of Midian, my brother Mosis is looking at the same disk.

I put on my dress and turn to look at Ramesses. I am surprised to see tears in his eyes.

"How do you say it in Habiru?" he asks. "*Hallelu Ya?*"

I am startled. All these years I have known him, and I did not know he knew any Habiru.

He smiles. "I have been trying to learn what I can, should that be the only language Batya will use with me—if I ever see her again."

I offer him my hand and help him get up. "Yes. *Hallelu Ya,*" I say. Praise God.

As we start down the steps to go inside and begin the new day, I stop and look at the sun. The god has survived another journey through the chaos of night. And so has Mosis.

So has Mosis.

Author's Note

THE NOVEL DEVELOPED far differently than I had anticipated. This was due primarily to the extensive research I did about ancient Egypt. What I learned was that the negative picture of Egypt given in the book of Exodus is not historically accurate. While it may reflect how the ancient Hebrew *felt* about the Egyptians, it distorts Egyptian civilization and culture. As I read and watched videos about ancient Egypt, I knew that I did not want to write a novel in which the Jews were the good guys and the Egyptians the bad. Human experience is more complex than that.

The challenge with any novel is how to tell the story. Which voice or voices will best communicate the time, the place, the people? I tried different points of view and voices—third person omniscient, first person using Batya—but neither worked. Then I wondered, *What about telling it from the point of view of Miriam, the sister of Moses who watches the basket in which the baby Moses is lying and offers to get a wet nurse for the baby after Pharaoh's daughter discovers it?*

I went back to the book of Exodus to reread the story and, to my surprise, found that Miriam is not mentioned. "Then said his sister to Pharaoh's daughter: 'Shall I go and call you a nurse of the Hebrew women, that she may nurse the child for you?' And Pharaoh's daughter said to her: 'Go.' And the maiden went and called the child's mother." (Exodus 2:7–9)

I looked in a concordance and found that Miriam is not mentioned by name until the crossing of the Red Sea: "And Miriam the prophetess, the sister of Aaron, took a timbrel in her hand; and all the women went out after her with timbrels and with dances. And Miriam sang to them...." (Exodus 15:20–21) Rabbinic exegetical tradition does not like people in the Torah to be nameless and bestows names or links people from different stories. Thus, finding a name for a sister in this story, the rabbis assumed it was the same sister who offered to get a nurse for her baby brother.

I did not make that assumption. Instead I asked myself, *Why didn't the Torah call Miriam by name from the beginning?* I reread Exodus 2:8, this time in Hebrew: "Va'tomer lah bat-Paro lechi va-telech ha-almah va-tikra et-aim ha-yeled." ("And the daughter of Pharaoh said to her, 'Go,' and the young girl of marriageable age went and called the mother of the child.")

When I read the word *almah*, "a young girl of marriageable age," the thought came: *What if Moses had a sister older than Miriam named Almah?* I knew I had the character and the voice through whom the story could be told.

Writing about a civilization that existed more than three thousand years ago is a challenge, to put it mildly. Yet, because the Egyptians left a visual record in the numerous tomb paintings as well as written records, we know a lot about ancient Egypt. All the names used are authentic, and I have sought to be historically faithful throughout and in ways that will not always be obvious. For example, ancient Egyptians had no concept of time smaller than an hour. That is why no character here says, "Wait a minute," and there are no descriptions saying, "She paused for an instant." (At least I hope that is the case. It is very difficult to write without measuring time as we are accustomed to doing.) The Egyptians did not have money, so I could not have a character ask, "How did you spend your day?" or use figures of speech using concepts involving payment, such as "He paid a price for what he did."

For those who might be bothered by the references to nudity, nudity was common in ancient Egypt. I did not include it to the extent that I could have, for fear that extensive inclusion would overshadow the book itself. Too, I was not writing a history book. This is a novel. As such, it is ultimately a work of the imagination. No one knows for sure what happened more than three thousand years ago when a people we call Egyptians and a people we call Hebrews encountered each other. We have the story as recorded in a sacred text, but sacred texts record sacred truths, not necessarily historical ones. My concern here is not sacred truths but human and psychological ones.

And human and psychological truths can illuminate sacred truth, revealing dimensions and facets that cannot be seen in any other way.

A word about how I have portrayed Moses: Besides the Torah, our ideas about who Moses was have been given to us by popular culture, namely two films, Cecil B. DeMille's epic *The Ten Commandments*, with Charlton Heston as Moses and Yul Brynner as Ramesses, and the animated film *Prince of Egypt*. Both depict Moses and Ramesses as brothers, and both also depict Moses as growing up and learning only later that he is Hebrew.

Historians believe that Ramesses the Great was the pharaoh referred to in the Torah. I decided to make him Moses' grandfather rather than his brother because the Torah also tells us that the Hebrews "built for Pharaoh store-cities, Pithom and Raamses." (Exodus 1:11) If the city named Raamses—Pi-Ramesses in Egyptian (House of Ramesses)—was built by the Hebrews before the birth of Moses, I concluded that Ramesses the Great was already on the throne and, therefore, could not have grown up with Moses as his brother.

The novel also reflects my long held view that Moses was the first person in history to grow up with a split identity, and attempts to resolve it through an act of violence. In my imagination Moses always knew he was Hebrew, but he loved being Egyptian. There is some confirmation for this in the Torah. When Moses flees Egypt and goes to the land of Midian, the daughters of the priest of Midian go to their father and say, "An Egyptian delivered us out of the hand of the shepherds...."

(Exodus 2:19) Obviously, then, Moses looked like an Egyptian and may even have identified himself to the daughters as an Egyptian. The Midrash says that one reason God did not permit Moses to enter the Promised Land or even be buried there was because he pretended to be an Egyptian when he went into Midian.

The toughest problem to resolve was Moses' speech. In translations Moses is described as a stutterer. But in the Hebrew, he describes himself as being "heavy of mouth and heavy of tongue." No one knows exactly what this means, but in Hebrew there are times when Moses' speech differs from occasions when he is repeating what God has told him to say. Sometimes when Moses is speaking for himself, the Hebrew has an almost primitive quality, a heaviness of mouth and tongue that is difficult to convey in English. One of the ironies of the Moses story is that the man God chooses to be the deliverer is also a man who has difficulty speaking. This detail adds a human dimension to the figure of Moses, which I have tried to convey through what sometimes sounds like pidgin English. One will not see Charlton Heston in my Moses.

One of the major problems in writing historical fiction is that of how did people talk? What distinctions existed between informal and formal speech? What were the colloquialisms and figures of speech? Often historical fiction errs in one of two ways—either the language is so stilted and formal that it bears little resemblance to an English that the reader can see himself in, or it disregards history entirely and uses modern slang that also distances the reader from the book. I have sought the middle ground by varying the formality and informality of language depending on who is talking and to whom. I am grateful to Professor David Van Blerkom, a colleague of mine at the University of Massachusetts who teaches astronomy and from time to time offers a seminar in hieroglyphs. He confirmed my sense that while the written Egyptian of sacred texts is formal, the spoken language was, for the most part, informal.

The "Hymn to Osiris" at the end of the novel is adapted from "Hymn to Osiris" in E. A. Wallis Budge's *The Dwellers on the Nile* (see the bibliography). I want to acknowledge Professor Helen Lefkowitz of the Classics Department of Wellesley College, whose e-mail correspondence, suggestions of books, collegiality, and responses to my questions and speculations were helpful during the research phase of this book. However, she does not share responsibility for any historical errors that may be found herein.

I also want to thank Rabbi Yechiael Lander, the now retired Jewish chaplain at Smith and Amherst Colleges. Back in 1979 when I spontaneously found myself writing about Bythia, the daughter of Pharaoh, I wondered if what I was writing was violating Jewish tradition. So I took what I had written to Rabbi Lander who, after reading it, smiled and explained, "This is midrash."—a way of exploring a text through the use of one's imagination. It is a time-honored tradition in Judaism. Rather than violating Jewish tradition, I was exemplifying it. Two years later Rabbi Lander would supervise my conversion to Judaism.

A warm thanks to my editor, Paula Wiseman, and her assistant, Rachel Goldberg, and everyone at Harcourt. You are a joy to work with.

Without the presence in my life of Milan Sabatini, my wife, best friend, companion, researcher, and at-home editor, neither I nor this book would be.

A final note: Like many people, I am not sure if I believe in reincarnation. But I have always found it interesting how people can be drawn to certain periods in history and not others. Ancient Greece and Rome have always bored me, whereas ancient Egypt feels like home in a deep sense. So, in writing this novel and feeling that I was writing my own story (in my identification with Almah), I couldn't help wonder if in a previous life I had lived in the time of Ramesses the Great.

Several months after finishing the novel, I was reading to my wife one evening as she lay in bed, a custom of ours. One of the books we are reading is the *Oxford English Dictionary*—all twenty volumes! On this particular evening I came to a word and, literally, chills went through me, leaving me unable to speak for several moments. Finally, still unable to speak, I slid the volume to my wife and let her read it for herself. The word was *almah*: "An Egyptian dancing-girl."

Glossary

PRACTICALLY ALL of our vocabulary regarding ancient Egypt, including the word *Egypt*, comes to us from either the Greeks or the Arabs. Where possible I have substituted the original Egyptian words for place names, months, deities, etc. I have also used Hebrew names for the more familiar English ones. As readers we bring our own historical and cultural contexts to what we read. Imagining oneself into history—as readers and writers—challenges us to leave behind as many of our associations as we can in an effort to understand the past, and in doing so, better understand ourselves. It is an act of respect we hope will be shown us when we are someone else's past. —J. L.

Abba   Hebrew for Father

Aharon   Hebrew for Aaron

Akhet   Name of one of the three Egyptian seasons. Akhet was the Season of the Inundation when the Nile flooded. It corresponds to the months of July through October.

Amon-Re   The primary deity of Egypt during the New Kingdom (1550–1070 B.C.E.)

Amram   The name given to the father of Moses by Jewish tradition.

Amu	Egyptian word for Hyksos, Asiatic peoples who lived in Egypt from 1640 to 1532 B.C.E. They introduced military weapons and the horse and chariot to Egyptian culture, and revolutionized agricultural methods.
Asetnefret	The actual name of the Second Royal Wife of Ramses. Her name is also sometimes spelled as Isetnefret.
Avraham	Hebrew for Abraham
Battle of Kadesh	A battle between a Hittite army and an Egyptian army led by Ramses the Great that resulted in a treaty between the two kingdoms. The courage and leadership Ramses showed in battle did much to establish his reputation among his own people.
Batya	Hebrew name for Bythia, the daughter of Pharaoh who took the baby Moses from the Nile River and raised him as her son
Book of the Dead	An ancient Egyptian book that gave instructions on how to survive in the afterlife to the deceased. These instructions were placed on the walls of tombs.
Chava	Hebrew for Eve
Esav	Hebrew for Esau
Eset	The Egyptian goddess we know by her Greek name, Isis
Festival of Opet	A New Year's festival held at the time the Nile flooded. It lasted for a month and was held at present-day Karnak and Luxor.
Gan Eden	Hebrew for the Garden of Eden
Goshen	The name of the region of Egypt where the Hebrews lived, as written in the Torah. See Genesis 47:4.
Great Green Sea	A translation of the Egyptian name for the Mediterranean Sea

Great Hapi Egyptian name for the Nile. It means "sweet water."

Habiru The ancient Akkadian name for the Hebrew people. Since there is no reference in ancient Egyptian records to the children of Israel, it is impossible to know how they were referred to in Egyptian. I chose an ancient word that was used for them. It is also spelled sometimes as Hapiru. The etymology is unclear, but it is possible that from this word came the Hebrew word *ivri*, "people from the other side," which is used in the Torah.

Hathor Egyptian goddess who was the protector of women and patron of love and joy and mistress of song and dance

Hittites An ancient people who lived in an area that is now Anatolia, Turkey, and northern Syria

Hor The Egyptian god Horus

Hor-em-akhet Egyptian name for the Sphinx

Ima Hebrew for Mother (pronounced Eee-mah)

isfet In Egyptian religion, the concept of injustice, violence, and chaos with which *maat* was in a constant battle to defeat

ka An Egyptian word with several layers of meaning: (1) the spiritual essence of a person that was the guiding force of life; (2) an astral being that existed alongside a person and had its own individuality; (3) an aspect of the divine essence on which all existence depended

Kakemour This is an ancient Egyptian male name. The character is invented.

Khemet	What the Egyptians called Egypt. It means "black land" because of the mud deposited by the annual inundations of the Nile. Upper Egypt, where the Nile is bordered on both sides by desert, was known as Red Land.
Maat	Both a goddess and the ancient Egyptian spiritual ideal. It is similar to the Taoist concept of Tao, denoting cosmic balance and harmony between earth, heaven, and humanity.
Merenptah	The fourteenth son of Ramses the Great; he became coruler during the latter years of Ramses's reign and succeeded him as pharaoh.
Meryeta-mun	One of the daughters of Ramses the Great and Nefertari. A statue of her is found at Abu Simbel, the temple built to mark the thirtieth year of Ramses's reign.
Miryam	Hebrew for Miriam
Mosis	Scholars agree that the biblical name Moses is a shortened form of an ancient Egyptian name, as in Tuthmosis. It is believed that the prefix of Moses' name was lost.
Nefertari	First Great Royal Wife of Ramses the Great. She was reputed to be a woman of extraordinary beauty and character. She died at about the thirtieth year of Ramses's reign. We know of his great love for her because of the statues of her at Abu Simbel. It was rare for a pharaoh to depict any of his wives. Also, Ramses had a temple built in her honor next to his own at Abu Simbel. Her tomb at Thebes is one of the most well preserved, and the wall paintings showing her are among the most remarkable tomb paintings that have survived.
Opet	Today known as the city of Thebes

Osiris	One of the central gods of ancient Egypt
Pi- Ramesses	The city built by Ramses the Great in the delta. It is referred to in the Torah in Exodus 1:11: "Therefore they did set over them taskmasters to afflict them with their burdens. And they built for Pharaoh store-cities, Pithom and Raamses." No ruins of the city remain, and its location is uncertain.
Ra'kha'ef	Pharaoh who reigned from 2520 to 2494 B.C.E. and built the second pyramid and the Sphinx at Giza
Ramesses II	Also known as Ramses the Great (1290–1224 B.C.E.) The longest reigning pharaoh, who lived to age 96 and is believed to have had more than 200 wives and concubines and sired 96 sons and 60 daughters. Some scholars believed he is the Pharaoh of the Bible.
Rivka	Hebrew for Rebecca
Sarah	Wife of Avraham
Season of the Inundation	See Akhet.
Shemu	The season of Harvest, corresponding to the months of March through June
shesheset	(Also known as *sistrum* or *seses*) Musical instrument associated with the goddess Hathor
Sutekh	The god Seth. The Egyptian name means "instigator of confusion," "the destroyer."
Taweret	The goddess of childbirth who was depicted with the body of a hippopotamus, the head of a crocodile or lion, and the feet of a lion. She was sometimes dressed in the robes of a queen.
tjat	"The robed one," or prime minister, as we would say today

Wadjet   Goddess who was the protector of Lower Egypt

Ya   One of the Hebrew names of God. The English word *hallelujah* is the anglicization of the Hebrew *hallelu*, "praise," *Ya*, "God."

Yaakov   Hebrew for Jacob

Yekutiel   According to Jewish tradition, the name Moses was given at birth.

Yitzchak   Hebrew for Isaac

Yocheved   According to Jewish tradition, the name of the mother of Moses

Bibliography

BOOKS

Andrews, Carol. *Amulets of Ancient Egypt*. London: British Museum Press, 1994.

―――. *Ancient Egyptian Jewelry*. London: British Museum Press, 1990.

Baines, John, and Jaromír Malék. *Atlas of Ancient Egypt*. New York: Facts on File Publications, 1996.

Barbarian Tides: TimeFrame 1500–600 B.C. Alexandria, Va.: Time-Life Books, 1987.

Budge, E. Wallis. *The Dwellers of the Nile: The Life, History, Religion, and Literature of the Ancient Egyptians*. New York: Dover, 1977.

Bunson, Margaret R. *A Dictionary of Ancient Egypt*. New York: Oxford University Press, 1995.

Gillispie, Charles Coulston, and Michel Dewachter, eds. *Monuments of Egypt: The Napoleonic Edition*. 2 vols. Princeton, N.J.: Princeton Architectural Press, in association with the Architectural League of New York and the J. Paul Getty Trust, 1987.

Hobson, Christine. *The World of the Pharaohs: A Complete Guide to Ancient Egypt*. New York: Thames and Hudson, 1987.

Kunz, George Frederick. *Curious Lore of Precious Stones*. New York: Dover, 1971.

Maitland, Sara. *The Ancient Egyptian Pack and Book*. Illustrated by Christos Kondeatis. Boston: Bulfinch Press, 1996.

McDonald, John K. *House of Eternity: The Tomb of Nefertari.* Los Angeles: Getty Conservation Institute and J. Paul Getty Museum, 1996.

Montet, Pierre. *Everyday Life in Egypt in the Days of Ramesses the Great.* Philadelphia: University of Pennsylvania Press, 1958.

Murnane, William J. *The Penguin Guide to Ancient Egypt.* London: Penguin, 1983.

Past Worlds: The London Times Atlas of Archaeology. New York: Crescent Books, 1995.

Patrick, Richard. *All Colour Book of Egyptian Mythology.* London: Octopus Books Ltd., 1972.

Reeves, Nicholas. *The Complete Tutankhamun.* New York: Thames and Hudson, 1990.

Robins, Gay. *Women in Ancient Egypt.* Cambridge, Mass.: Harvard University Press, 1993.

Scamuzzi, Ernesto. *Egyptian Art in the Egyptian Museum of Turin.* New York: Harry N. Abrams (no date).

Scholz, Piotr O. *Ancient Egypt: An Illustrated Historical Overview.* Hauppauge, N.Y.: Barrons Educational Series, 1997.

Stead, Miriam. *Egyptian Life.* Cambridge, Mass.: Harvard University Press, 1986.

Steedman, Scott. *Ancient Egypt.* New York: DK Publishing, 1995.

Tyldesley, Joyce. *Daughters of Isis: Women of Ancient Egypt.* New York: Viking Penguin, 1995.

Unstead, R. J. *See Inside an Egyptian Town.* London: Kingfisher Books Ltd., 1986.

Yoyotte, Jean. *Treasures of the Pharaohs.* Geneva: Skira, 1968.

What Life Was Like on the Banks of the Nile: Egypt 3050–30 B.C. Alexandria, Va.: Time-Life Books, 1996.

PERIODICALS

Arden, Harvey. "In Search of Moses." *National Geographic* (January 1976): 2–37.

Dothan, Trude. "Lost Outpost of the Egyptian Empire." *National Geographic* (December 1982): 739–769.

Gore, Rick. "Ramses the Great." *National Geographic* (April 1991): 2–31.

Johnson, Electa and Irving. *"Yankee* Cruises the Storied Nile." *National Geographic* (May 1965): 583–633.

Kendall, Timothy. "Kingdom of Kush." *National Geographic* (November 1990): 96–125.

Miller, Peter. "Riddle of the Pyramid Boats." *National Geographic* (April 1988): 534–550.

Roberts, David. "Age of Pyramids: Egypt's Old Kingdom." *National Geographic* (January 1995): 2–43.

Simpich, Frederick. "Along the Nile, Through Egypt and the Sudan." *National Geographic* (October 1922): 379–410.

VIDEOCASSETTES

The Giant Nile. Blue Bird Films, 1990.
The Great Pharaohs of Egypt. A&E Television Networks, 1997.

WEB PAGES

Ancient Egyptian Virtual Temple. http://www.netins.net/ showcase/ankh/index.html

Encarta Interactive World Atlas Online. http://www.encarta.com/ewa/pages/a/42297.htm

Tour Egypt. http://touregypt.com

The Great Temple of Abu Simbel. http://www.ccer.ggl.ruu.nl/ abu_simbel

University of Chicago Epigraphic Survey. http://www-oi. uchicago.edu/OI/Mus/PA/EGYPT/Egypt_AbuSimbel.html